THE GOLDEN POMEGRANATE

Folktales of Azerbaijan

Volume I

by **Rustam Musevi**

Hazar Global Press

The Golden Pomegranate: Folktales of Azerbaijan, Volume I

Written and adapted by **Rustam Musevi**

Published by Hazar Global Press

St. Paul, Minnesota, USA

Library of Congress Control Number: 2025919070

ISBN: 979-8-9994622-0-6

Cover design and illustrations by Rustam Musevi

Printed in the United States

Second Edition: 2025

To the storytellers of my childhood,

and

the children who will carry the stories forward.

Map of Azerbaijan

This decorative map is a symbolic representation of the region. Not to scale.

Contents

Prologue

I've felt nostalgic for the warm nights of my childhood, tucked under the duvet, listening to my aunts read from an old book of Azerbaijani folktales. I'd drift off to sleep as the stories from those worn pages slipped into my dreams, carrying me to faraway lands where imagination ran free. Years later, I became consumed with reading folktales from around the world, often in my grandma's quiet room. That childhood wonder never left me, and it's what inspired this collection. Years later, I've returned to those same tales, reimagining them in English so new generations might feel the magic I once did.

I grew up in a bilingual home and a multicultural society. Years later, almost without realizing it, I found myself raising my own children the same way. But this time, the challenge was greater: keeping a heritage alive in a land far from where it began. In the US, children's worlds are shaped in the English language. Even when they grow up hearing their parents' native tongue and learning about their heritage at home, many still struggle to fully connect with it.

For those who don't, the stories risk fading further with each new generation. I needed to retell those stories in a language that is better understood by the latest generation. I have taken on the challenge to modernize it in a way that connects with parents and children. I wasn't just translating stories into English; I was also deliberately annotating the moral lessons that would motivate, inspire, and encourage young readers to be like the heroes in the book.

The folklore of Azerbaijan, often referred to as the Land of Fire, brings to life characters who face seemingly impossible challenges, make tough decisions, and consistently remain empathetic, kind, and generous. These timeless qualities are cherished in every culture worldwide. I hope the folktales of Azerbaijan introduce readers around the world to the colorful folklore of the Land of Fire. This is not only about preserving heritage for those with roots in Azerbaijan, but rather about sharing stories that resonate with the human spirit, regardless of where you live or what language you speak.

Folktales are more than just old stories. They carry values, humor, lessons, and the spirit of a land. The folklore characters I grew up with were part of every child's world in Azerbaijan. But to new generations, especially those growing up abroad, they risk becoming strangers. That's why I've chosen to retell these tales, not simply to translate them, but to reimagine them in modern English, while keeping their heart and cultural richness intact. My goal is to bring these centuries-old stories back to life for a wider audience, so that children and families, whether in the US or any other part of the globe, can read them, enjoy them, and carry them forward.

This is Volume I of *The Golden Pomegranate: Folktales of Azerbaijan*, a collection for curious minds, young readers, and anyone who believes in the power of a good story. I hope you find something familiar in these pages… and something new to love.

The Clever Fox

Long ago, deep in an untamed forest, a lion and a tiger were the best of friends. They did everything together; hunting, resting, and roaming the woods side by side. Their bond was so close that the other animals could only watch with envy.

But no one was more jealous than the fox. Clever, sly, and always plotting, she hid in the bush day after day, her sharp eyes fixed on the happy pair.

"Why should they be friends," she muttered to herself, "while I have no friend?" She thought and schemed about how she could break up their friendship.

Every morning, the tiger rose before dawn and headed off to hunt while the lion slept peacefully. One day, the fox finally came up with a plan. She waited until the tiger had gone hunting, then crept over to the lion, looking as miserable as possible.

"Brother Lion," she said sadly, "there's something I want to tell you, but I fear you won't believe me."

"Speak," said the lion. "I will decide whether to believe you."

The fox lowered her voice and whispered:

"I heard from another animal that tomorrow morning he might challenge you, just to prove everyone who's really king of the forest."

"Bah, nonsense!" laughed the lion. "We've been friends since we were cubs. I know him better than anyone."

"Believe me or not," sighed the fox, "but wait until morning. You will see the truth for yourself."

Though the lion tried to brush it off, a seed of doubt was planted in his mind.

"What if...?" he thought. "No, it cannot be... but I will watch him carefully just in case."

Meanwhile, the fox slipped away and went searching for the tiger. She found him not far off and, putting on her most worried face, said:

"Brother Tiger, I need to tell you something, but I am afraid you won't believe me."

"Tell me," said the tiger. "If it is true, I will believe it."

The fox sighed deeply.

"You walk through these woods, and all the animals admire your strength... but I heard something odd. Someone said your friend the lion is planning to challenge you, just to prove who's really king of the forest."

"Nonsense!" said the tiger. "The lion? We are as close as brothers!"

"I knew you wouldn't believe me," said the fox, shaking her head.

"But just wait until tomorrow morning, when you see him raise his paw in a move like he is ready to challenge you, you will know I wasn't lying."

The tiger did not fully believe the fox either, but he grew uneasy.

"Better to be ready," he thought.

That night, neither the lion nor the tiger slept well.

At the first light of dawn, both woke up, tense and watchful. The lion yawned wide, stretching as he always did, raising both paws high into the air. But the tiger, already tense and full of doubt, saw something else entirely.

"He is getting ready to strike!" the tiger thought.

Without a word, the tiger leaped at the lion. After a moment of shock, the lion fought back. They battled fiercely, clawing and biting, until both fell lifeless to the ground. The fox watched the scene from behind a tree with a sneaky smirk.

When the dust had settled and the forest was silent again, she ran off to gather all the other foxes. They gathered around, marveling.

"How did you manage to turn such good friends into enemies?" they asked.

The clever fox grinned.

"I watched, listened, and planted the right seeds of doubt. The rest took care of itself."

Though her plan had worked perfectly, the clever fox did not feel the joy she expected. With a sigh, she wandered back into the woods, looking for something more, though even she wasn't sure what.

Not far from the forest, in a small hut, lived two hunters: Pirim and Mamed. They were closer than brothers — they did everything together. When the fox heard about the two hunters and how close they were, her ears perked up.

"Everyone talks about their friendship like it is something special," she scoffed. If I could tear apart a lion and a tiger, two humans should be easy."

So, she limped up to their hut, pretending to sob.

"Oh, dear brothers," she cried, "please help me! My family was hunted down by wolves and bears! I ran for my life and barely got away! Please let me stay, and I will be your eyes and ears! I will track animals and birds for you and warn you of danger."

Mamed, a kind-hearted man, took pity on her and let her stay. But Pirim was suspicious.

"Watch out, Mamed," he said. "Foxes are sly. You can never trust them."

For a few days, the fox lived with them, quietly spying. She noticed something in their morning routine she could use for her clever plan. Each morning, Pirim would step outside, string his bow, and shoot a few arrows into the trees before carefully setting it aside.

Meanwhile, Mamed would walk down to the creek to splash his face with cold water, then lift a heavy stone and toss it aside with a grunt, just to keep strong. Neither hunter knew the other's habits. The fox chuckled to herself.

One morning, the fox went up to Pirim.

"I have something to tell you," she said, pretending to weep. "But you won't believe me."

"Say it anyway," said Pirim.

The fox sniffled and whispered:

"This morning, I heard Mamed bragging that he is the better hunter, and stronger, too. He laughed and said, 'Tomorrow morning, I will show Pirim what real strength looks like with that stone I toss every day.' I would keep an eye on him, just in case."

Pirim's eyes widened.

"Impossible! Mamed is my closest friend!"

"I knew you wouldn't believe me," said the fox. "But just watch out tomorrow morning. He will go to the stream, act innocent, and throw a stone at you."

Pirim did not believe her entirely, but a seed of doubt took root inside him.

Meanwhile, the fox ran to Mamed.

"Brother," she said breathlessly, "I must tell you something, though you may not believe it."

"What is it?" asked Mamed.

The fox lowered her voice.

"I overheard Pirim this morning, saying he is a better hunter than you and said, 'Tomorrow morning, Pirim, will see how fast my bow is before he can pick up that stone."

Mamed laughed.

"Impossible! Pirim would never do that."

"Believe me or not," said the fox, "but tomorrow morning, you will see him ready his bow and aim at you. If I am lying, you can cast me away indefinitely."

Mamed did not fully believe her either, but like Pirim, he decided to keep an eye out.

At sunrise, each hunter quietly kept an eye on the other, just as the fox had warned. Pirim reached for his bow; not to attack, but simply as part of his morning routine. Still, Mamed's heart pounded. "Is this it?" he wondered.

At the same time, Mamed walked down to the stream and picked up a heavy stone, just like always. But Pirim, tense with doubt, thought, "he is going to throw it at me, just like the fox said."

Each saw exactly what the fox had described. Their tempers boiled over. They nearly attacked one another, but just in time, they stopped and decided to talk.

"Friend," said Pirim, "I see anger in your eyes. What has happened?"

They sat down and shared everything the fox had told each of them. In the end, they realized the truth: The fox had tricked them both.

"If we believed her lies," said Mamed, "we could have ended up destroying one another."

They decided it was time to teach the fox a lesson. Pirim and Mamed grabbed each other by the shoulders and pretended to wrestle, falling to the ground as if dead. Watching from the bushes, the fox thought her plan had worked again! She skipped over, clapping her paws.

"Fools!" she laughed. "Just like the lion and the tiger! You've fought each other until you both end up flat on the ground!"

But just as she stepped closer, Pirim sprang to his feet, grabbed her by the tail, and with one swift motion, spun her through the air and sent her flying far beyond the edge of the forest.

And that was the end of the clever fox, at least in that part of the forest.

No one saw that fox again, though now and then, when the wind rustled the leaves just right, the animals would whisper:

A whisper of doubt, if planted deep, can turn friends into enemies.

The Crane and the Frog

Long ago, one warm afternoon, a tall crane was sipping water at the edge of a quiet marsh when a little frog peeked her head out from the muddy water.

"Hello, Brother Crane," the frog croaked cheerfully. "Why don't we become friends?"

The crane paused and looked down at her kindly.

"I'm not sure that would work," he said gently.

"Why not?" asked the frog, tilting her head.

"Well," replied the crane, "you live down here in the water, and I spend my days flying high up in the sky. I cannot visit you under the water, I'd drown. And you do not have wings to come flying with me."

The frog thought for a moment and then said, "That is okay! Whenever you come by the water's edge, I will hop out to see you. That way, we can still talk and enjoy each other's company."

The crane smiled. "All right," he said. "Let's give it a try."

And so, they did. The crane would often stop by the pond during his travels. He and the frog would sit and chat about the skies, the water, and the world. They became good friends in their own special way.

One day, during one of their talks, the frog suddenly said,

"Brother Crane, I've lived in this swamp all my life. I've never seen anything beyond it. But you ...you fly so high. You've seen the mountains, the rivers, the fields, and the towns. Will you take me with you someday and show me the world?"

The crane blinked. "But... how would that work? You do not have wings."

"I do not need wings," the frog said excitedly. "You could carry me between yours. I will hold on tight!"

The crane hesitated. "It's dangerous. You might fall."

But the frog wouldn't give up. She begged and pleaded until the crane finally gave in.

"All right," he sighed. "But hold on tightly."

He gently lifted the frog onto his back, tucked her between his wings, and began to rise into the sky.

They soared just above the pond when the frog, overcome with excitement and wonder, looked down. To her surprise, she lost her grip.

Down she tumbled, flipping and tumbling through the air, until she landed with a splash in the swamp. Mercifully, she landed in the water and survived, although she was a bit bruised and shaken. The crane quickly glided back down and landed beside her.

"I warned you, Frog," he said with a soft shake of his head. "Some friendships, while well-meant, are not always easy. As the old saying goes; friendship between two very different creatures can sometimes lead to trouble."

Friendship is a beautiful thing, but even among friends, it's wise to know your limits.

Hungry Bear

ong ago, in a vast, whispering forest that had stood for centuries, there lived an old bear with fur as gray as morning mist. When winter arrived, snow fell thick and heavy, covering the trails and hiding the roads.

One by one, the animals of the forest tucked themselves away into their warm dens to sleep through the cold months. But the old bear? He could not find rest. His belly ached with hunger, so he wandered the silent woods, searching and searching for something to eat.

One day, weary from his fruitless wandering, the bear lay down and fell into a deep sleep. And in his dreams, he saw a beautiful sight: a tender, juicy slab of meat. It felt so real, his mouth began to water.

The bear woke suddenly, convinced that his dream was a sign from fate. Surely, somewhere out there, this meat awaited him! Without hesitation, he crossed mountains and valleys, driven by hunger and hope.

At last, he came to the foot of a mountain where a shepherd tended his flock. One foolish goat, straying from the others, wandered into the bushes. At that very moment, a great stone rolled down the mountain, striking the goat and knocking him to the ground.

The bear, prowling nearby, wasted no time. He lunged toward the helpless creature.

"Aha, little fella," he growled, his eyes gleaming. At last, my dream has come true! I shall eat you before you can even bleat!"

The poor goat tried to flee, but the stone had squished his leg. There was no escape, and as the bear prepared to pounce, a clever thought flashed through the goat's mind.

"Dear Brother Bear," said the goat in a sweet voice, "I know you mean to eat me. But allow me, I beg you, one last kindness. Let me sing my final song as a farewell to this world."

This piqued the bear's curiosity, and he agreed. And the goat began to sing, a mournful, sorrowful song echoing across the hills. Hearing the strange cry, the shepherd immediately understood that trouble had found his flock. He seized his staff, called his dogs, and rushed to the rescue.

The old bear, catching sight of the shepherd and the fierce dogs bounding toward him, turned tail and fled into the forest. He wandered hungrier and weaker with every step until he came across two black rams. The rams, seeing that they could not outrun him, bowed low and said:

"Good day to you, Brother Bear! Is the forest treating you kindly today?"

"Kindly? Hardly!" the bear growled." I have roamed these woods hungry for a week. But now, at last, I find you two, and I will eat you both and fill my belly!"

Yet the two Rams were no fools.

"Brother Bear," said one, "eat me first."

"No!" cried the other. "Eat me first!"

The bear, annoyed by their arguing, declared:

"Settle it between yourselves. Fight! And whoever loses his horns first, he shall be my meal."

That was precisely what the rams had hoped! They backed away, pretending to prepare for battle, and then, together, they charged straight at the bear. With a terrible crack, they struck him between the eyes. The world spun black. The bear collapsed to the ground, stunned. And when he awoke, the rams were long gone. Groaning, battered, and bruised, the bear staggered on. In a narrow gorge, he spied a beautiful horse. Joy filled his heart.

"Better than a goat! Better than two rams!" Thought the bear. "When I feast on him, even the wolves will envy me!"

He chased after the horse, but the gorge was too narrow for escape. The horse, seeing there was no hope, turned to the bear and said:

"Brother Bear, I know you will eat me. But grant me this one mercy: I do not want to see it. Let me turn away."

The bear, eager for his meal, agreed. He circled behind the horse, opened his mouth wide to bite, but the horse was clever and strong. The horse lifted his leg quickly and kicked the bear.

Struck by the horse's swift kick, the bear stumbled and collapsed into the snow, stunned and breathless. By the time he rose, the horse was gone, and the gorge was empty.

Miserable and broken, the old bear limped on. At last, he met a fox. The fox, seeing the battered bear, could hardly contain her laughter.

"What has happened to you, Brother Bear?" she asked slyly.

And the bear, heavy-hearted, told her all his misfortunes. When he finished, the fox laughed and said:

"Well, dear Brother Bear, after all you've been through, I doubt you will dream of a big meal anytime soon!"

With that, the bear sighed, shook his aching head, and shuffled into the snowy forest. There, he soon found a quiet cave to rest and drift into deep sleep through the winter.

The Tale of the Hungry Wolf

ong ago, there was a wolf who roamed the hills and valleys, gobbling up every sheep and goat in sight. Yet no matter how much he ate, he was always hungry.

One day, a lion and a tiger were traveling together. They walked a long way, rested, then walked even farther, until they arrived at the wolf's den. When they stepped inside, they found the wolf lying on his side, groaning.

The tiger asked,

"Hey there, Brother Wolf. How are you?"

The wolf moaned,

"Not good. I have not eaten a thing in three days. I'm starving."

The lion said,

"Then come with us. Maybe we will find something to eat along the way."

But the wolf groaned louder.

"I want to, but I cannot. I am too weak to stand up."

The tiger said,

"No worries. Stay here and rest. We will bring you something by lunchtime if we find anything."

As soon as they left, the wolf jumped to his feet and slipped out the back to his secret food stash. There, he pulled out the two lambs he had hidden earlier, sniffed the meat with a twitch of his nose, let out a satisfied "Mm!", then tucked the lambs back into their hiding place. He returned to his den, rolled onto his side, paws over his belly, pretending to be the hungriest, saddest wolf in the forest.

Meanwhile, the tiger had split off from the lion and gone out in search of food. After some time, he came to a riverbank where a fisherman had dozed off, leaving several large fish by his side. The tiger looked left and right, no one in sight, grabbed the fish, and ran all the way back to the wolf's den.

"Brother Wolf," he said, panting, "Here, eat these fish to help you regain your strength."

The wolf smiled. "Thank you, Brother Tiger. You saved my life."

As soon as the tiger left, the wolf chuckled to himself.

"This is brilliant. I don't even have to lift a paw. These fools will hunt and bring me food. I've found the perfect job."

He stored the fish next to the lamb meat and strolled off to visit his neighbors. First, he went to the rabbit's garden.

"Hey Rabbit," the wolf growled, "I have seen you munching those juicy melons, but you never share."

The rabbit replied nervously,

"But Brother Wolf, there are only a few good melons this year. I barely have enough for myself."

The wolf snarled, "I do not care. You'd better bring me my share."

Next, he paid a visit to the golden pheasant.

"It has been ten days," he snapped, "and not a single chick from you. What kind of neighbor are you?"

The golden pheasant fluffed her feathers. "I don't have any chicks right now."

"Well, find some," the wolf barked. "Or I will take all of your eggs."

Meanwhile, the tiger ran into a fox who was gnawing on a dry old bone.

"Why are you gnawing on a dry bone, Uncle Fox?" the tiger asked. "The meat's long gone."

"Isn't it obvious?" the fox replied.

The tiger sat down beside him. "I see. You are hungry, just like the old wolf I knew. He was starving and I just gave him some fish."

The fox burst out laughing.

"What's so funny?" the tiger asked.

The fox grinned.

"If I had just one piece of the lamb meat that old wolf has hidden in his den, I would be full for a year!"

The tiger's eyes narrowed.

"No way. That cannot be true."

"Then let's bet on it," said the fox. "Let's go check out the wolf together."

So, the fox and the tiger began walking to the wolf's den. Along the way, they met the lion, and the tiger told him what the fox had revealed. The lion joined them. Then they ran into the golden pheasant, who said,

"That old wolf eating our food, leaving us with nothing!"

"See?" said the fox. "That's one."

Further down the road, they met the rabbit. He, too, complained bitterly about the wolf.

"That's two," said the fox, smirking.

The tiger sighed.

"I guess you were right, Fox."

Now the whole group—fox, tiger, lion, rabbit, and golden pheasant—marched straight to the wolf's den.

The moment the wolf saw them coming, he clutched his belly and collapsed onto the ground, pretending to be weak from hunger.

"How are you, Brother Wolf?" asked the tiger.

The wolf groaned, "I think I am going to pass out from hunger."

Then he closed his eyes and faked his own death, hoping they would go away.

But the fox stepped forward.

"Our dear brother wolf lived a hard life. Let's give him a proper burial."

They quickly dug a deep hole.

"Come on," the fox said. "Let's cry a little for our poor wolf brother."

They all pretended to cry. The wolf kept his eyes shut, waiting for his chance to escape. But the fox leaned close and whispered to the tiger,

"It's time to lay our brother in the ground."

They lifted the wolf and dropped him into the grave. As soon as he landed, the wolf sprang up and dashed away, never to be seen again in that part of the forest.

Then the fox said,

"Now, let's find the wolf's pantry."

They found his secret stash with lamb meat, fish, and more.

They feasted and then went on their way.

Don't mistake kindness for weakness. Sooner or later, even the cleverest trickster gets caught.

The Mouse and the Cat

Long ago, a mouse and a cat lived together in a cozy little cottage at the edge of the woods, where their uneasy friendship was always one meal away from trouble. One day, the mouse peeked out of his hole and said to the cat,

"Let's be brothers."

The cat raised an eyebrow. "That won't work," he replied.

"Why not?" asked the mouse, surprised.

"Well," the cat said, "You are a coward, a thief, and a troublemaker. That is not what I am looking for in a brother."

"I admit I am a little timid," said the mouse, "but I am no thief or pest."

The cat smirked. "Oh really? Aren't you the one who chews through sacks and steals flour and grain?"

"And you, brother cat, do you not eat too?" the mouse countered. "Don't eat, too?"

"I ask politely. I meow, and the humans give me meat and bread. But you—you just take whatever you want without asking."

After going back and forth like this for a while, the cat finally said, "Fine. Let's be friends. But if you ever lie to me or steal, do not say I did not warn you; I will eat you."

The mouse was delighted. From then on, they lived together.

One day, the mouse had an idea.

"Brother cat," he said, "it's autumn. The weather's still good, and there's food all around. But winter's coming. Soon, the snow will fall, and food will be hard to find. Let's start storing food now."

"Good idea," said the cat.

"You know," said the mouse, "I'm not exactly welcome in people's homes. If I try to gather food, they might kill me. But you—they love you. If you meow near a house where they're churning butter, they'll toss you a bit. You could collect a whole stash."

The cat agreed and soon gathered a plentiful supply of butter. They found a clay pot, filled it with the butter, and buried it under a tree in the garden.

As winter neared, temptation got the better of the mouse.

"Brother cat," he said one day, "my cousin is having a baby-naming celebration. I've been invited. May I go?"

"Go ahead," said the cat, "but do not be long."

The mouse ran straight to the tree, dug up the pot, ate a bit of the butter, covered it back up, and returned home.

"What did they name the baby?" asked the cat.

"Little-Bitty," said the mouse.

"Nice name," the cat replied. "But what does it mean?"

"Not sure yet," said the mouse. "Two more cousins are getting named soon. I will explain all three together."

A few days passed. The mouse got hungry again.

"Brother cat," he said, "I have been invited to another cousin's naming. I really cannot skip it. Family would be upset."

"Go," said the cat. "Just come back quickly."

The mouse raced back to the garden, ate until the pot was halfway empty, buried it again, and returned.

"What's this cousin's name?" asked the cat.

"Halfway," the mouse said.

"Your family picks such strange names," the cat murmured.

A little while later, as the weather turned colder, the mouse panicked. Soon, snow would cover the garden, and the cat would never find the pot again.

"Brother cat, one last cousin. Please let me go. After this, no more."

The cat nodded. "All right. Just do not stay too long. I get lonely."

The mouse dug up the pot, licked it clean, and buried the empty jar. When he got back, the cat asked, "And this cousin's name?"

"All-Gone," the mouse replied.

The cat smiled.

"What's so funny, brother cat?" the mouse asked. "Do you not like the name?"

"Oh, I am just wondering what they all mean," the cat said. "I suppose I will understand once I see the pot."

Brother cat, I am tired," the mouse protested. "Let's do it tomorrow."

"Tomorrow, then," the cat agreed.

The next morning, the cat was eager. "Come on, brother mouse. Time to check our butter."

The mouse tried again to stall, but the cat wouldn't hear it. Together they went to the tree, dug up the pot, and found it empty.

"You…sly little sneak!" the cat roared. "You ate the butter!"

"I did not," the mouse lied. "You must've eaten it yourself."

"How could I have eaten it?" the cat snapped. "Explain!"

"Well," said the mouse, "maybe you ate 'Little-Bitty,' then 'Halfway,' and finally 'All-Gone.'"

The cat's eyes narrowed. "Those names… I know them. That is what you told me your cousins were called!"

"That is right," said the mouse. "And now you know what they mean."

"I do," the cat growled. "You lied, you stole, and you broke your promise. And what did we agree on? If you ever tricked me, I would eat you."

"But we are friends, brother cat!" the mouse pleaded. "Friends do not eat each other!"

"You are right," said the cat calmly. "Friends don't. But thieves and liars who do not change their ways, they do not get a second chance."

And with a quiet sigh, the cat leapt forward, and the little mouse was gone, just as they had once agreed.

Friendship is built on honesty and trust. If you lie and steal, even your closest friend may turn away.

The Clever Boy

ong ago, a cruel and greedy khan ruled the land with tyranny. He constantly found excuses to invade nearby towns and villages, forcing them to pay exorbitant taxes.

But near his city was one village he couldn't conquer, because it was full of wise elders who could outsmart his every attempt at conquering it. Frustrated, the Khan gathered his advisors to come up with a plan.

"As long as those elders are alive," said his Vizir, "that village will never be yours. First, we must get rid of them."

The Khan liked that idea. That very day, he sent his men to the village with a fake request: "Our khan is facing a terrible problem," they told the elders. "He needs your advice just for one day."

The elders did not trust them, but in the end, they agreed to go. As soon as they arrived, the Khan had them all thrown in prison.

Then he gave a rider three apples and an order. "One of these apples is from this year's harvest, one from last year, and one from two years ago," he said. "Take them to the village and tell the people: if they do not figure out which is which in three days, I will take over their land. But if someone does solve the riddle, they must come to me with my favorite animal. And one more thing: that person must be taller than me, so I would look up to him."

The rider galloped off, gathered the villagers, and delivered the message.

No one could solve the riddle.

In that same village lived a clever and brave boy named Ahmed. He stayed up all night trying to solve it but could not. In the morning, he asked his grandmother if any of the wise men still lived in the village.

"There's one old man still alive," she said. "He is so frail that the khan's guards did not bother with him."

Ahmed rushed to the edge of the village and found the old man, blind and bent with age. Ahmed greeted him politely and asked for advice.

The old man thought for a long time. Then he explained how Ahmed could tell the apples apart. "But one part I cannot help with," he added. "You will have to find out for yourself what the khan's favorite animal is."

Determined, Ahmed set off toward the Khan's city. Near the city walls, he had to stop. Guards stood every hundred steps and let no one in. Although people were unable to pass the guards, he noticed that flocks of sheep passed the guards freely.

Ahmed ran to some local shepherds and asked them to butcher a ram and give him its clean hide. They did. He wrapped the sheepskin in a cloth, waited by the trees, then pulled it over himself and crawled among the sheep right through the gates.

Inside the city, Ahmed saw a shepherd resting under a tree. Nearby was a goat so dazzling it did not seem real; its horns were gold, a golden bell hung from its neck, and its back was covered in fine cashmere. Ahmed couldn't take his eyes off it.

"Why are you staring?" the shepherd asked.

"I have never seen a goat like that in my life!" Ahmed said.

"You must not be from around here," the shepherd replied. "Everyone knows this is the Khan's favorite goat. He has loved goats since he was a boy."

Ahmed now had the answer he needed. He sneaked back out the same way he came, disguised as a sheep, and returned to his village, where people had lost all hope to find an answer for Khan's ultimatum.

On the third day, Ahmed stood up in the main square and said, "Give me a camel and a goat. I will go to the Khan and solve the riddle."

The Khan's guards brought Ahmed before the Khan. At first, the Khan was furious to see only a boy. But then he noticed the goat and fell silent. Ahmed had already answered part of the riddle.

"You were supposed to be taller than me," the Khan sneered.

"But I am," Ahmed replied. "You are talking to me while I sit on a camel. you are looking up."

"Yes," the Khan admitted. "But if you step down, you will barely reach my waist."

"Then why should I step down?" said Ahmed with a smile.

The Khan scowled. "Fine. Let's hear your answer about the apples."

Ahmed stood tall. "I will only answer in front of your people. Bring them to the town square."

The Khan did not like it but decided to go with it. He warned, "If you are wrong, I will throw you in prison with the elders."

"I accept," said Ahmed.

A platform was built. The people gathered. The Khan arrived in his finest robes.

"If I solve your riddle," said Ahmed, "You will release our elders and leave our village alone. If I am wrong, do as you will."

The Khan nodded. Ahmed asked for a bowl of water. He dropped the three apples in. One sank to the bottom. One floated in the middle. One bobbed on the surface.

"The apple that sank is from this year, it's full of juice and heavy," Ahmed explained. "The one in the middle is last year's, it has dried a little and lighter. The one floating is from two years ago, so dry it barely weighs anything."

The crowd gasped. The Khan stayed silent. He did not want to keep his promise, but he was afraid of losing face in front of such a large audience. In the end, he gave in. He released the imprisoned elders and promised not to touch the village again.

Ahmed returned home with the wise men, and the whole village came out to greet the boy who had outsmarted the cruel Khan. From that day on, his name stood for courage and wit. Years later, children still told the tale of the clever boy who defeated power with nothing but a ram's skin, a cup of water, and the truth.

You do not need might to stand for what's right— when truth is your weapon and wisdom your guide, even the fiercest power cannot stand.

The Wise Old Man

Long ago, in the far corners of the world, there lived a cruel and heartless Shah. Under his law, when a parent's back is bent by age and their steps slow, the children are required to carry them to a distant place in the hills, say a final goodbye, and leave them there forever. This cruel custom, enforced by the Shah, had gone on for years, and no one dared to question it.

One day, a young man named Ibrahim saw that his father had grown too weak to walk. Knowing what the law demanded, he said:

"Come on, Father. It is time. I cannot delay any longer."

The old man sighed, his eyes heavy with sorrow.

"As you wish, my son. It is your decision."

The family said their tearful goodbyes, and Ibrahim placed his father into the woven basket and lifted him onto his back. Step by step, they made the sad journey toward the hills. As they walked, the father let out a deep, heavy sigh. Curious, Ibrahim asked why, but the old man said nothing. Ibrahim kept pressing him until, at last, the father said:

"I was just remembering the day when I carried my own father down this same road... just as you are doing now."

His words hit Ibrahim like a bolt of lightning. Guilt filled his chest. He wanted to turn back, but he was afraid to break a law. So, he kept walking, slower now, with a heavy heart.

When they reached the hills, Ibrahim set his father down and paused to rest. The old man looked at his son and said gently,

"Go home, my son, but do not forget to take the basket."

Confused, Ibrahim replied,

"Father, this is the same basket I used to carry Mother. You are the last elder in our home. Why would I need the basket anymore?"

His father looked him in the eyes and said,

"You have a son too. One day, he will grow up, and you will grow old. He will use this same basket to carry you here."

Ibrahim froze. His entire body trembled. It was like waking from a terrible dream.

Suddenly, he cried out, "No, Father! I won't abandon you!"

He jumped up, looked around, and noticed a cave hidden at the base of the hill. He carried his father inside and said, "Stay here, Father. I will bring you food and blankets. I will take care of you."

He stacked stones at the cave entrance to block the wind but left space for light and air. True to his word, Ibrahim visited every day, bringing food and water and keeping his father warm and safe.

Sometime later, a terrible problem struck the city. A dragon had appeared at the source of the city's river and blocked the flow of water. No one in the town had a single drop to drink. The people were desperate.

Warriors and heroes tried to fight the dragon, but none could defeat it. Whoever came near was burned to ash by the dragon's fire. The Shah made a royal announcement:

"Whoever drives the dragon away or kills it will receive half of my royal treasury!"

But no one dared challenge the beast again.

Meanwhile, Ibrahim was visiting his father as usual. He brought food—but no water. His father noticed and asked,

"My son, why did not you bring any water today?"

Ibrahim explained,

"A dragon is blocking the river. No one in the city has any water. The Shah has promised a great reward to anyone who can stop it, but everyone who tries is burned alive."

The old man thought for a moment. Then he said calmly,

"I can help defeat the dragon."

Ibrahim's eyes lit up.

"If you can do that, Father, you will save the whole kingdom! The Shah will reward us with treasures beyond measure!"

His father smiled and said,

"Go to the shah. Tell him to build a giant mirror, ten arshins tall and four arshins wide. Have the people hold it from behind and carry it toward the dragon. When the dragon sees its own reflection, it will be frightened and think another monster is coming. It will panic and run. Chase it with the mirror until it leaves our land."

Ibrahim rushed to the palace.

"Your Majesty, I can defeat the dragon, but only if you keep your promise!"

Desperate from thirst, the Shah agreed and swore an oath:

"You will have half my treasury if you succeed. Take whatever you need!"

Ibrahim had the mirror made exactly as his father described. People held it from behind and carefully approached the dragon's lair.

The dragon saw the reflection, a terrifying beast spewing fire, and thought it was a rival creature coming to kill. In a panic, the dragon turned and ran.

Each time it looked back, it saw the same monstrous image following it and ran faster. The people chased it, holding the mirror until the dragon fled the Shah's land entirely.

Water flowed back into the city. The people cheered and danced in the streets. The Shah summoned Ibrahim and asked:

"Tell me, how did you come up with such a brilliant plan?"

Ibrahim replied,

"Your Majesty, this was not my idea. No matter how wise the young may be, they will always need the wisdom of the old. We must protect and respect our elders, not throw them away like broken tools. It was my father who gave me the idea and saved us all."

The Shah was stunned. The people fell silent, listening in awe. The Shah commanded:

"Bring this wise old man here!"

A crowd rushed to the hills and brought the old man to the palace. The Shah gave Ibrahim half of his treasure, just as promised, and more importantly, he abolished the cruel custom.

From that day forward, the elderly were treated with kindness and care. No more baskets. No more hills. The wisdom of the old was once again treasured, because what they know may one day save our lives.

The wisdom of the old is the light of the young.

The Tale of Baldy and The Judge

Long ago, in a lively city where dusty roads twisted through noisy markets and busy crowds, there lived a judge. He was wealthy, important, and well-known across the land for mistreating others. The Judge was always hiring new helpers, but none stayed longer than a week. Some were left aching and sore from harsh treatment and overworking. Others were scolded until they gave up and walked away.

To anyone who passed by, the Judge would say, "I need a hardworking servant." But even the most willing workers were quickly worn down by the Judge's never-ending demands and sharp tongue.

One of his former helpers, a young man named Iman, had just returned to his village. Tired, bruised, and glad to be free, he sat under a tree to rest. Just then, a neighbor strolled by; a lanky, cheerful fellow everyone called Baldy. His head shone in the sun, and he always had a clever twinkle in his eye.

"Why would you leave the judge's house?" Baldy asked with curiosity.

Iman sighed. "He mistreated me, worked me from morning till night, and tossed me out like an old broom. I am telling you, even if a saint worked for him, they wouldn't last a week."

Baldy grinned. "Then I will go and see for myself. I want to meet this Judge who cannot keep a servant."

"Do not do it," Iman warned. "He'll have you aching from head to toe before the week is out!"

But Baldy shrugged. "If he wants help, he will have to make a promise not to mistreat me."

That evening, Baldy went home and packed some bread into a satchel. "Mother," he said, "I am off to find work in the city."

His mother looked him over and frowned. "In those patched-up trousers? You will be laughed at before you reach the gates!"

But Baldy only chuckled, tossed the bag over his shoulder, and set off on his way toward the Judge's house and whatever adventure waited beyond its gate.

Baldy walked for hours beneath the sun, his patched trousers flapping in the wind and his bag of bread swinging at his side. At last, he reached the Judge's grand house, a tall building with wooden gates and a garden full of pomegranate trees. He knocked. The door creaked open, and the Judge stepped into the courtyard, his eyes narrowing.

"What do you want?" the Judge asked.

"I heard you are looking for a hardworking helper," Baldy replied with a friendly bow. "Well, here I am."

The Judge looked him up and down. "Hmm. How did you know? I do need someone. The last one quit just yesterday." He stroked his beard. "I will pay ten silver coins a month. And if you work hard, I will add five more next month."

Baldy nodded. "Fair enough. But let's settle things now so we do not argue later."

"What do you mean?" the Judge asked.

"I had a father," Baldy said softly," and I loved him dearly. Suppose you agree never to insult him, not even once. I will work hard and say nothing in return. But if you do curse my late father, you will owe me five silver coins for every insult. You must write and sign a promise."

The Judge chuckled. "That is all? Fine. Bring me paper."

And so, the Judge signed the promise with a flourish, never guessing what sort of servant Baldy would turn out to be.

From that day on, Baldy worked from dawn until dusk. The Judge sent him here and there, fetching water, chopping wood, tending the garden, and more. Baldy worked cheerfully, though he never hurried. He sang to himself as he swept, hummed as he carried baskets, and always seemed to have a sparkle in his eye.

One morning, the Judge called out, "Baldy! I am going to stay at my orchard outside the city. Bring me water in the large jug with the broken handle."

Baldy searched the courtyard for this old jug. He looked behind the shed, under the stairs, and even peeked into the well house. But no jug with a broken handle could be found.

So, what did Baldy do?

He went down into the cellar, found a brand-new jug, and snapped off the handle himself. Then he gave it a little chip on the rim for good measure, hoisted it onto his shoulder, and set off toward the orchard.

When the Judge saw the jug, his eyes nearly popped out of his head.

"My new jug! What have you done?" he roared.

Baldy stood calmly. "You asked for a jug with a broken handle. I couldn't find one, so I made one."

The Judge's face turned as red as a pomegranate. He clenched his fists, bit his tongue, and tried to hold back the storm brewing inside him. But it did not last.

"You donkey! You ruin everything! And your father must have been twice as foolish as you!"

At that, Baldy reached into his pocket and pulled out the folded promise.

"That is five silver coins for the insult, good Judge," he said, smiling sweetly.

The Judge turned pale. He had forgotten all about the deal. Just then, a calf wandered into the orchard, munching leaves as it walked.

The Judge saw it and barked, "Grab that calf by the tail and bring it here!"

Without a word, Baldy did as he was told. But he pulled with such force that the poor calf's tail came right off in his hand.

Baldy held it up. "You asked for the tail. Here it is."

The Judge opened his mouth to yell but stopped. He glared at Baldy, then shouted, "Get out of my sight, you troublemaker!"

But Baldy did not leave. He crossed his arms and stood firm.

Soon, the shouting drew a crowd: neighbors, workers, and even a few curious children. They watched as the Judge fumed, and Baldy calmly unfolded the paper again.

"Let's count," Baldy said. "You insulted my father exactly one hundred and eighty-eight times. Five silver coins for each insult that makes," he paused for effect, "nine hundred and forty silver coins."

The people gasped. They read the paper and saw the Judge's signature.

"He must pay!" they said. "A promise is a promise!"

The Judge was red with embarrassment and shaking with anger. But there was no way out, not without losing face.

"Come," he said through gritted teeth. "We will go to the city and settle this properly."

On the way to town, the Judge grumbled the whole time. He kept glancing sideways at Baldy, who was cheerfully humming a tune and skipping stones as they walked.

When they passed a small pasture, the Judge suddenly snapped, "Baldy! Get my donkey from the field. And make it quick!"

Baldy nodded and ran off. But the donkey, feeling playful, darted into a nearby vegetable patch.

"Grab him by the neck and pull him out!" shouted the Judge.

Baldy cupped his hands around his mouth. "Did everyone hear that?" he called to the nearby fieldhands. "The judge says: grab it by the neck!"

Then, just as instructed, Baldy pulled and the donkey's head twisted so far that it went limp. The poor animal collapsed to the ground. The Judge shouted in disbelief.

"You broke its neck!" he yelled. "That was my favorite donkey!"

"But you told me to do it," Baldy replied, holding up the reins. "I followed your command exactly."

People began to gather again. Some laughed. Others shook their heads. A few whispered, "Is this Baldy lucky, or is he just clever?"

The Judge was beside himself. "You! You troublemaker! I will never pay you a coin! Not one!"

"Oh, I think you will," said Baldy calmly. "If not, I might have to take something else instead."

"You wouldn't dare!"

Baldy gave a dramatic sigh. "Then perhaps your cow? Seems fair, since your words cost you silver, and your donkey," he paused, "well, that was on you."

The crowd was growing.

"Give him what you owe!" someone called out.

"He has the paper!" shouted another.

"Do not make it worse, Judge!" a third added.

The Judge realized the crowd was not on his side.

Just then, Baldy took a deep breath and was about to say something more when a tall man stepped onto the road. He wore a cloak of midnight blue, his hair hung long and black, and his eyes sparkled like the stars.

"Where are you going in such a hurry?" the man asked Baldy kindly.

"I am chasing a runaway judge," Baldy said. "And who are you?"

The man smiled. "I'm what you refused to curse. I am the very one people blame when things go wrong."

Baldy blinked. "You are… the cursed one?"

"Not quite," the man said with a wink. "Just a bit of magic people do not always understand. Let me show you."

And just like that, he whispered a few words and Baldy's face changed. His nose curved differently, his hair grew out, and even his voice deepened. He looked nothing like himself. Then, the stranger turned himself into a donkey.

"A fair trade," said the magic donkey. "Ride me to the Judge. Offer me for sale. Just do not hand him the reins."

Baldy nodded, mounted the donkey, and trotted back to the Judge's house with a sly smile on his newly borrowed face. The Judge had barely made it home when he heard hoofbeats outside his gate. Peeking nervously through the shutters, he saw a stranger riding the most handsome donkey he had ever laid eyes on. Its coat gleamed, its ears twitched alertly, and it moved with the grace of a gazelle.

The Judge forgot all about Baldy.

He rushed outside. "What a fine animal! Is it for sale?"

The rider dismounted and nodded. "It is two hundred silver coins."

"Done!" the Judge said without a second thought. He went back inside, returned with a heavy pouch, and counted every coin into the stranger's hand. "You drive a hard bargain, friend, but that donkey's worth it."

"Just one thing," said the rider. "Do not touch the reins too quickly. He is sensitive."

The Judge barely heard him. He was already leading the donkey into the stable, beaming with pride. Meanwhile, the stranger, who was, of course, Baldy, tucked the coins into his coat and strolled away, whistling.

Back in the stable, the Judge poured fresh barley into the feed bin. "Eat, my beauty, eat!" he said with pride. The donkey bent its head, but instead of eating, it stuck its nose into a gap between the wooden planks and couldn't pull it back out. The Judge pulled. He pushed. He twisted. Nothing worked.

 Finally, frustrated, he yanked the donkey's tail with all his strength, and the tail came off in his hands. Before he could scream, the donkey gave a final hee-haw! and vanished through the wall like smoke. The Judge stumbled backward, still clutching the tail, wide-eyed with shock. He burst out of the stable, shouting, "Thief! I've been tricked! I've been robbed!"

At that moment, a breathless messenger from the Shah's palace burst in. 'Honorable Judge!' he cried. 'The Vizir needs to see you right away!'"

Still dazed, the Judge dusted himself off and hurried to the Vizir's palace. He straightened his robe, smoothed his mustache, and entered the great hall with all the dignity he could gather. But he couldn't hide his frown.

"You look troubled," said the Vizir. "Something wrong?"

The Judge sighed. "It's too ridiculous to put into words."

"Try me."

The Judge explained how he bought a magnificent donkey, how it vanished into the wall, and how only the tail remained.

The Vizir raised an eyebrow. "And who sold you this magical donkey?"

The Judge squinted. "I might have seen him near your gate…"

The Vizir snapped his fingers, and the guards brought Baldy in.

The Judge jumped to his feet. "That is him!"

Baldy shrugged. "I have never seen this man before."

The Judge waved a paper. "Here is your handwriting and sale receipt!"

Baldy leaned forward, looked at the paper, and chuckled. "That? That is not a receipt. That is a playing card. Your Honor must've mixed up his papers."

Guests gathered, murmuring. Someone took the paper and held it up. "He is right. It is just a card."

"Ridiculous!" the Judge cried. "He gave me the donkey's tail too!"

He reached into his cloak, but when he pulled his hand out, it wasn't a tail he held. It was a saz, a long-necked string instrument, like an old mountain cousin of the guitar, often used to play folk stories.

The guests burst into laughter.

"You are carrying musical instruments and gambling cards?" someone teased.

"He is not a judge," said another. "He is a traveling clown!"

The Judge's face turned a deep shade of purple with embarrassment.

"Wait!" he shouted. "He also gave me the donkey's horseshoe!"

He reached into his other pocket and pulled out another playing card.

Everyone roared. Even the Vizir smirked. "I think the youngster wins this round."

And with that, the Vizir dismissed Baldy with a wave.

The boy bowed politely, then skipped off toward the Judge's house, where he gathered up his belongings and everything the Judge owed him. Then, with the pouch of silver swinging on his hip and a song on his lips, Baldy made his way back home.

Back in his village, Baldy's return caused quite a stir. Children gathered around to hear about the vanishing donkey and the Judge's dancing rage. Elders chuckled behind their beards, and even the grumpiest farmer smiled at the clever lad's tale.

Baldy, gave his mother half the silver and used the rest to patch his pants, fix up their old house, and buy two real donkeys with sturdy tails.

The Judge never hired another servant again. Some say he still peeks into stables, muttering about disappearing donkeys and magical musicians. Others say he learned to be a little less cruel and a lot more careful with his words. But everyone agrees:

That was the day a poor boy in patched trousers outwitted a man in velvet robes and got paid fair and square.

Ahmed the Porter

ong ago, in a bustling city rich in trade and color, lived
a wealthy merchant. Every morning after breakfast, he would walk to
the market to check on the latest goods and see how business was going.
Thanks to his sharp eye and deep pockets, the best items always found
their way to him.

One day, the merchant bought a large haul of goods and packed them
into a massive chest. He began searching for someone to help carry it.
Soon, he spotted a young man sitting nearby.

"Hey there," the merchant called. "I need someone to lift this chest onto
a cart, bring it to my shop, unload it, and carry it inside."

The young man, Ahmed, stood up and looked at the chest.

"Tie it up and help me get it on my back," he said. "I will carry it myself."

"Are you crazy?" the merchant replied. "You will break your back! This
thing is too heavy even for three men to lift. We need a cart."

Ahmed shrugged. "Do not worry about me. You just show me where to
take it."

With the help of three bystanders, the chest was hoisted onto Ahmed's
back. Then, to everyone's amazement, he walked down the road with it
as if it were light as air. The merchant barely kept up.

At the shop, Ahmed set the chest down and sat for a moment to rest. The merchant noticed the young man's strength and suddenly had an idea.

"If I bring him to the Shah," the merchant thought, "I could earn a fortune. The Shah is looking for strong warriors."

When Ahmed stood to leave, the merchant stopped him.

"You are not going anywhere," he said. "You are coming with me to the Shah's palace."

Ahmed waved him off. "The palace? The Shah? What do I have to do with all that? Just let me go. Keep your money."

But the merchant insisted, dragging him to the king. When the Shah saw Ahmed, tall and strong with broad shoulders, he was amazed.

"We could use that kind of strength in my army," he said.

He immediately gave Ahmed fine clothes and shining armor. The merchant was rewarded with gold and sent home. Ahmed moved into a large room in the palace. He locked up his old porter clothes in a chest, slipped the key into his pocket, and stepped out into the royal gardens. That is when the Princess first saw him and fell in love. Ahmed saw her, too, and felt the same. They wanted to speak to each other but did not know how.

The next day, Ahmed returned to the garden, hoping to see her again. He strolled around, but she wasn't there. Feeling sad, he turned to leave, but then he saw her gracefully walking beneath the canopy of trees that lined the rose-filled garden. They greeted each other shyly, spoke for a while, and opened up to each other. From then on, they met often in the garden, but trouble came soon. A giant dragon appeared at the source of the river, cutting off the city's water. The Shah called his warriors.

Ahmed knew what was coming. He took out his chest key, changed back into his old clothes, and tried to sneak out. Just then, the princess caught him.

"Where are you going?" she asked. "Everyone believes in you. It is your moment. You must fight the dragon!"

"Why me?" Ahmed replied. "What do I have against a dragon? I would rather go back to carrying boxes."

She begged him. "Send the army ahead. Wait nearby. When the battle starts, hide. Then come back once it is over."

Ahmed hesitated but agreed. He changed into his armor, took his place at the head of the army, and marched out. At the river, he commanded the soldiers to attack, then lay under a tree to rest. But as he dozed, the dragon crept toward him. Seeing its monstrous head, Ahmed sprang up, drew his sword, and, with one mighty swing, sliced the beast in two. The army cheered and rushed to tell the king. Ahmed was brought back to the palace, where he was honored with gifts from the people.

"Did not I tell you?" said the princess. "You were never in danger. Now ask my father for my hand in marriage."

The Shah agreed. Ahmed and the princess were engaged, and the palace buzzed with wedding preparations. But then, news came: a second, even larger dragon had blocked the river. The Shah called Ahmed again. Ahmed sighed, pulled out his key, and returned to his old clothes. The princess rushed in.

"You cannot run now! We are engaged!"

"That is exactly why I am running," he said. "I barely survived the first one. I am not risking my neck again."

She begged again: "Climb a tree this time. Nobody will notice you."

Reluctantly, Ahmed agreed. He put on his armor, led the army again, and when the battle started, climbed the tallest tree and tried to sleep. But the dragon smelled him. As it approached, Ahmed struck with all his strength and cut off its head. Cheers erupted again. Ahmed was hailed a hero. The princess ran to embrace him. Soon, a date was set for their wedding. But just before the celebration, war was declared by a rival Shah.

"Prepare for battle," said the Shah. "The wedding must wait."

Ahmed groaned. "I'm not a soldier. I am done risking my life!"

Again, the princess calmed him. "Ride a quiet horse. Stay back. you will be safe."

So, Ahmed looked for the weakest horse, tied himself to it so he wouldn't fall, and set off. But the horse was no ordinary nag — it was the Shah's fastest steed. Spooked by a whip, it bolted into battle. As it raced forward, Ahmed grabbed a massive tree and held it like a club. He crashed into enemy ranks, knocking them down like twigs. Terrified, the enemy fled. The army returned, lifting Ahmed high in triumph.

The wedding lasted forty days and forty nights.

And when the Shah once asked, "Why did you tie yourself to the horse?"

Ahmed replied, "Because I promised myself: I would either return a victor, or not at all."

And so, he did. The story reveals that true courage is quiet but rises when needed, even in those who doubt themselves.

The Tailor's Apprentice

Long ago, in a sun-drenched land of domes and minarets, there lived a tailor with nimble hands and thread that never knotted. He stitched robes for the townsfolk—simple, sturdy, neat.

But one day, a royal guard knocked loudly at his door.

"Come with us," the guard ordered. "The Shah has summoned you!"

The tailor packed his finest clothes and followed the guard to the palace, his heart thumping like a drum beneath his vest. The Shah sat high on a golden cushion, his robes shimmering like moonlight on silk.

"I want a robe," the Shah said, "unlike anything the world has ever seen. Bring it to me by sunrise tomorrow or lose your head at dawn."

The tailor bowed low, sweat dampening his brows.

"I will do my best, Your Majesty."

Back at his shop, he called to his apprentice, a bright-eyed boy who had learned to thread a needle before he could write his name.

"We have work to do," the tailor said. "A robe for the Shah. It must be wondrous, or we will not live to stitch another seam."

By candlelight, they worked, hour after hour, cutting, folding, and stitching stars into sleeves, sewing moonlight into the hem. The night deepened. The wind whispered through the shutters. The apprentice's head began to droop.

"Stay awake, boy!" the tailor said. "If we fail, it is our necks!"

"I'm awake," the boy mumbled, but his eyelids were heavy as stone.

The candle flickered as the boy stirred, blinking away sleep.

"Stay awake, boy!" the tailor said. "If we fail, it is our necks!"

"I'm awake," the boy mumbled, but his eyelids were heavy as stone.

The candle flickered as the boy stirred, blinking away sleep.

"Were you dreaming?" the tailor asked, noticing the faraway look in his eyes.

"I did," the boy whispered. "Just for a moment."

"Well? Tell me. What did you see?"

The boy hesitated. "I cannot say it yet. I will only tell you when it comes true."

The tailor raised an eyebrow, his expression both amused and annoyed. "So be it. But stitch faster, or it will not matter what you dream."

And stitch they did. All through the night, through shadows and silence, until the first pink threads of dawn crept over the rooftops.

The robe was finished, light as a breeze, glowing with threads like sunlight and fire. It shimmered with patterns no one could name, geometries born of dreams.

The tailor wrapped it in silk. "Take this to the Shah," he told the boy. "Be brave, and whatever happens, hold your head high."

The apprentice bowed and walked through the still-sleeping streets, his heart beating louder with each step toward the palace gate. The guards let him in. The Shah waited, cloaked in gold and shadow.

"Have you brought the robe?" he said, eyes narrowing.

"I have, Your Majesty." The apprentice unfolded the bundle.

The robe unfurled like a sunrise. The Shah's breath caught. "Magnificent!"

He touched the fabric, admiring the detail, then turned to the boy with a curious smile. The tailor had quietly informed the Shah that the apprentice had not slept all night, only dozed off for a moment and dreamed of something strange.

"Now," said the Shah, surprising the apprentice, "tell me about your dream."

The boy stood firm. "I will tell you, Majesty, when the dream becomes real."

The Shah's face darkened. "How dare you defy me? Do you forget that I am the Shah?"

"I gave my word," said the boy, "and I must keep my promise."

Fury flickered in the Shah's eyes. "Then you shall sit in the deepest cell until you change your mind."

He waved his hand. The guards seized the boy. Down he went, into the stone belly of the palace, into the cold silence of the dungeon. But the apprentice did not weep or beg. He thought, "Not yet. The time will come."

The cell was dark, but the boy's eyes had grown used to shadows. Days passed slowly, like honey dripping from a cold spoon. Every morning, the Shah called for the apprentice and addressed him with the same proposal:

"Reveal the dream or remain in chains."

And each time, the boy answered softly,

"I cannot tell yet, not until the time is right."

Then back he went, through the winding halls, to the damp walls and silence of his prison. But this prison had a secret. One wall, rougher than the rest, hummed faintly when the wind blew.

The boy pressed his ear against it. On the other side, he heard music. Strings of a harp-like instrument called qanun, whispering a gentle tune, soft laughter, and the rustle of silken robes.

He listened again. That was no ordinary room beyond the stone. It was the garden chamber of the Shah's daughter. By moonlight, the apprentice was able to pull a loose stone from the wall and then another. His fingers were scraped and sore, but he worked quietly and patiently.

Finally, the opening was large enough for him to squeeze through. He slipped through the narrow space and found himself in a room glowing with lanterns. On a golden bed lay the Princess, her black hair fanned across the pillows like a night river. At her head and feet, her maids slept lightly.

However, beauty was the last thing on the apprentice's mind, and he was too hungry to care. He came for food. His stomach growled at the sight of a silver plate, still warm with saffron rice and lamb. He ate quickly, quietly, licking his fingers clean. Then, like a shadow, he slipped back through the wall and into the dark.

When the Princess opened her eyes the next morning, her plate was empty. Someone had eaten her food. The maids swore they had not touched the plate, but the Princess wasn't fooled. After a moment of quiet thinking, she whispered, "Someone's been here. Not a thief, but someone very hungry."

The same strange event repeated itself the next night, and the night that followed. On the third night, the Princess stayed awake. She hid behind a curtain, watching the plate of food. She waited… and waited…and then she saw him—dusty, wide-eyed, and barefoot. He stepped from the shadows, reached for the food, and began to eat.

In a flash, she stepped forward and grabbed his arm.

"Who are you?" she whispered, eyes wide with curiosity and surprise.

The apprentice dropped the spoon.

"I'm the tailor's apprentice," he said. "Forgive me."

He told her everything: the robe, the dream, the Shah's anger, and the prison cell. The Princess listened and did not call for guards. Instead, she smiled.

"You are brave and smart," she said.

Then she looked around to make sure no one was nearby.

"I will help you," she whispered, "but you must help my father too. His pride may be mighty, but his throne is fragile. The world is watching."

One bright morning, a royal messenger galloped into the capital, his banner dusty from the road. Without a word, he stepped into the city square and drew a perfect circle in the dirt using the tip of his stick of the stick.

"This," he announced, "is a message from the great Shah of our land. If your ruler is wise, let him explain what it means. If not, prepare your armies."

The people stared. A circle? What could it mean? Was it a threat? A puzzle?

The Shah gathered his advisors, scholars, and even poets.

They argued and whispered, but no one could decipher the silent message. With a face clouded with confusion, the Shah turned to his daughter.

"You are smart, my child. What do you see?"

The Princess studied the circle from the palace balcony. "It means war," she said calmly. "The circle stands for the world, and our enemy is claiming it all."

The Shah's face grew pale.

"But there may still be a way to answer wisely," she continued. "Call for the tailor's apprentice from the prison."

The guards hesitated, but soon, the young man was brought before the throne once again.

"You," said the Shah, "solve this riddle, and I may reward you. Fail, and well… Do not fail."

The apprentice bowed and replied, "I can answer it, but I ask something first."

The room fell silent.

"What is it?" said the Shah.

"If I succeed," said the apprentice, "you must give me your daughter's hand in marriage."

Gasps echoed through the palace. The Princess only smiled faintly, as if she'd expected this all along. The Shah looked from his daughter to the young man and finally gave a reluctant nod.

"Very well. Speak."

The apprentice turned to the city square. In front of the crowd, he walked up to the circle and drew a line through its middle.

"This," he said, "means the world must be shared. Half for your people and half for the other kingdom."

The crowd murmured, impressed by his calm. The foreign messenger nodded but said nothing. Instead, he placed a bow and arrow in the center of the circle.

"A challenge," whispered the Princess from her balcony. "They threaten war."

The apprentice stepped forward. "Then bring me a sword."

When the blade was placed beside the bow, he announced, "And this is our answer: We are not afraid to defend our half."

The messenger poured a sack of tiny grains into the circle.

"He says their army is as countless as these grains," the Princess called down.

The apprentice smiled. "Then bring me a rooster."

A freckled-feathered rooster was placed at the edge of the circle. It tilted its head, then began pecking furiously at the grain. The people laughed and clapped. The messenger's face turned red. He bowed stiffly, then left without a word. The riddle had been answered.

So, the apprentice was not only released from prison but praised throughout the land for his wisdom. And as for the Princess, her smile said everything.

Not long after the dust of the last challenge had settled, another envoy arrived from the neighboring Shah. This time, he carried no riddles made of words or symbols, but instead, a single object: a plain wooden stick.

He bowed low before the court and said, "Our Shah presents this wooden stick. He asks your wise court to answer one simple question: which end is the top, and which is the bottom?"

The Shah frowned. "It's just a stick. How can one tell?"

The court fell silent once again. Ministers and magicians scratched their heads. Philosophers squinted at the stick, but none could find an answer. The Shah sighed and turned to his daughter once again. "You always see more than others. Tell me what to do."

The Princess replied, "Ask the apprentice."

By now, the apprentice lived not in the prison but in the palace, near the Princess's rooms. He was brought before the Shah, who said, "Solve this puzzle, and name your reward."

The apprentice bowed. "My reward is already here," he said, glancing toward the Princess. "But I will need a stream."

"A stream?" asked the Shah.

"Yes," said the apprentice. "We'll let water decide what is high and what is low."

Soon, the court gathered beside a shallow stream that ran through the palace garden.

The apprentice walked to the water's edge and, without hesitation, tossed the stick into the stream. Everyone leaned in as the stick floated, bobbed, and slowly began to tilt. One end dipped beneath the surface while the other rose toward the sky.

"There," said the apprentice, pointing. "The end that rises is the top, and the end that sinks is the bottom."

The foreign envoy was speechless. He had no answer to that.

The Shah clapped his hands and smiled. " Wisdom and humility are more powerful than any army."

And though no wedding had yet taken place, the apprentice and the Princess were already speaking as one.

Word of the apprentice's cleverness spread beyond borders like wind through the mountains. The neighboring Shah, humiliated twice, grew bitter. His pride had been wounded, and he longed for revenge.

One day, he sent a message sealed with gold:

"Let the young man who solved the puzzle come to my court. I have one final task for him, if he dares."

The apprentice agreed. Before departing, he visited the Princess. She gave him a letter wrapped in silk and said, "Give this to the Shah's daughter when you arrive. Trust her wisdom."

The apprentice set off and soon stood before the foreign Shah. The ruler's eyes burned with a cold intensity.

"I hear you are very clever," he said. "Then sew me a robe of solid rock. If you cannot, you will lose your head."

The court gasped. The task was impossible. But the apprentice did not flinch.

He bowed politely. "If that is your wish, I will begin right away. But I will need a thread made from pure sand."

The Shah narrowed his eyes. "Thread from sand? That is impossible."

The apprentice smiled. "Exactly. Just as impossible as sewing a coat from stone."

There was silence. Then, the Shah's daughter, having read the Princess's letter, stepped forward. She had understood everything.

"This young man speaks true," she said. "Wisdom cannot be forced. Justice cannot be mocked."

The neighboring Shah had no answer. But in his heart, he knew he had been defeated once again. He let the apprentice go with gifts, gold, and deep respect.

The seasons passed, and the apprentice became a prince by marriage, living in peace and prosperity. He and the Princess had two sons: one as bright as the morning star, the other as gentle as the moonlight. Their home was filled with laughter, wisdom, and the quiet joy of a life well-earned.

One evening, the old Shah visited them. He stepped into the room where the apprentice sat with one child on each knee.

The Shah smiled softly. "You still haven't told me your dream."

The apprentice looked up, eyes warm with mischief and memory. He stood, bowed, and finally said:

"In my dream, I sat with a star on each knee… and the sun shining over my head."

The room fell silent. Then the Shah let out a deep, heartfelt laugh.

"That dream was worth the wait," he said.

From that day forward, the young man who once sewed robes in silence was known widely not just for his wisdom but for his patience, loyalty, and heart.

The tailor's apprentice, now prince, never returned to his needle and thread, but he never forgot the quiet strength they taught him how small stitches can hold great things together.

People from far and wide came to the court not only to admire the wisdom of the Shah but to seek the counsel of the young prince whose riddles once baffled kings. They did not see just an apprentice who answered impossible questions; they saw a clever man who had stitched his destiny with courage and kindness.

As for the dream? It lived on as a story, constantly reminding young hearts that sometimes the best answers come with patience, and a dream worth waiting for.

Twitty-Hanum

Long ago, there was a little bird named Twitty-Hanum. One sunny day, she flew out for a stroll and landed on a wild rose bush, singing her sweet song: "Twitt-Twitt!"

But just then, she pricked her tiny foot on a thorn. No matter what she did, she couldn't pull it out. Poor Twitty-Hanum began to cry in pain.

An old woman passing by heard her and asked:

"Oh, sweet little Twitty-Hanum, why are you crying?"

Through her sobs, Twitty-Hanum answered:

"Oh, Grandma, I am in trouble! A thorn stuck in my foot, and I cannot get it out. Please help me!"

The kind old woman gently pulled out the thorn and tossed it into the fire. Twitty-Hanum felt a wave of relief. She flitted around happily for a bit but then flew back to the old woman and chirped:

"Grandma, give me back my thorn."

The old woman laughed.

"How can I give it back? I threw it into the fire, and it is long gone."

But Twitty-Hanum insisted:

"You owe me. If you won't give it back, I will take a loaf of bread from your oven instead!"

The old woman chuckled and waved her off. But quick as a flash, Twitty-Hanum swooped around, grabbed a hot loaf of bread, and flew off into the sky!

Flying high above the fields, Twitty-Hanum spotted a shepherd milking his sheep. She swooped down and chirped:

"Good day to you, brother shepherd!

I've brought you a loaf of bread and have it with your milk."

The shepherd smiled, took the loaf, crumbled it into a bowl, poured milk over it, and said:

"Come, little bird, share the meal with me!"

But Twitty-Hanum shook her head.

"I'm not hungry. You enjoy it."

The shepherd finished the bread and milk. Just as he wiped his hands, Twitty-Hanum fluttered her wings and said:

"Now, brother shepherd, give me back my loaf."

The shepherd looked puzzled.

"How can I give it back? I ate it. It is gone."

Twitty-Hanum puffed up:

"You owe me. If you do not return my loaf, I will take one of your sheep!"

The shepherd laughed:

"Sweet little Twitty-Hanum, how is that my fault? You gave me the bread yourself. I just ate it!"

But before he could say anything, the bird zipped one way, zipped another, grabbed a sheep with her tiny claws, and flew away.

The poor shepherd shouted after her:

"Oh no! What will I tell the master? He will be furious!"

Twitty-Hanum flew on, clutching the sheep, when she spotted a group of horsemen galloping across the land.

She called out:

"Hey, brothers, where are you headed?"

The riders answered:

"Sweet little Twitty-Hanum, we are taking a bride to the palace for her wedding!"

Twitty-Hanum followed them straight to the palace gates. She knocked and handed over the sheep to the palace servants.

"Here's a wedding gift!" she chirped.

Then she perched proudly in the courtyard, right among the honored guests. The servants roasted the sheep, made juicy kebabs, and served the guests.

They seated Twitty-Hanum next to a goose and brought them a tray of kebabs. But the greedy goose gobbled up everything, leaving poor Twitty-Hanum hungry.

Furious, she fluttered up to the Great Shah and demanded:

"Give me back my sheep!"

The Shah's men replied:

"The sheep is gone. We ate it."

Twitty-Hanum stamped her little foot:

"I do not care! You took it from me, and you owe me! If you do not return it, I will take the bride!"

Everyone burst into laughter. Twitty-Hanum zipped away, perched on the garden wall, and waited.

The music started, and the bride stepped forward to dance, and quicker than the blink of an eye, Twitty-Hanum swooped down, grabbed the bride, and flew off! The Great Shah pulled at his hair, crying and wailing.

Twitty-Hanum carried the bride to a shady spot under a tall tree. There, she heard an Ashug playing his saz and singing.

The little bird called out:

"Good day, brother Ashug!

I will give you this bride if you give me your saz!"

The ashug's eyes lit up.

"Sweet little Twitty-Hanum, you can have anything you want! Take my saz!"

Twitty-Hanum handed over the bride and took the saz. The ashug led the bride home, happy as could be.

And Twitty-Hanum?

She sat on a bush and play the saz, singing:

I lost a thorn but found some bread,

Play, my saz, lift your head!

I gave the bread and won a sheep,

Play, my saz, dance, and leap!

I traded the sheep for a lovely bride,

Play, my saz, sing far and wide!

I gave the bride for a saz to play,

Play, my saz, all night and day!

From that day on, Twitty-Hanum played her saz and brought joy to everyone she met. Sometimes, it takes a few missteps, even a little mischief, to discover where we truly belong. Though she once deceived others, in the end, Twitty-Hanum found the music that gave her life meaning.

Bahtiyar's Journey

The Dream

Long ago, in a quiet corner of the world, lived a poor man named Bahtiyar. One morning, he woke up early and said to his wife:

"Listen, woman, pack me some barley bread and a little cheese. I am going on a journey."

His wife scolded him:

"Stay home, old man! Where would someone your age go wandering?"

But Bahtiyar insisted:

"Be quiet, old woman. I had a good dream, and I am going to find it."

"Ha! You've lost your mind!" she cried. "Whoever heard of chasing after a dream?"

"Just do as I say," Bahtiyar said firmly.

So, his wife packed the food, and Bahtiyar slung the bag over his shoulder and set off. He walked for a day and a night, then another day and another night, until he lost track of time altogether. Finally, he came to a wide-open steppe. There, he saw a shepherd with a large flock of sheep, a dog, a donkey, and a tent filled with the gear of nomads.

Bahtiyar approached the shepherd, bowed, and said:

"May your flock grow and prosper! There's an old saying: 'When you are hungry, seek out a shepherd.' Will you feed a tired traveler? My bread is so hard it is like stone!"

The shepherd, true to his kind-hearted reputation, quickly milked some sheep and handed Bahtiyar a bowl full of fresh milk. Bahtiyar crumbled his hard bread into it, ate gratefully, and began preparing to move on.

The shepherd asked:

"Kind stranger, where are you from, and how far are you going? If it is a long journey, I can give you some cheese and butter to take with you."

Bahtiyar replied:

"My friend, I am from such-and-such village. As for where I am going, I do not know myself. I've lived a hard life, but I had a dream not long ago. It was such a beautiful dream that I decided to go find it."

The shepherd was surprised.

"Find a dream? People dream a thousand dreams every night. How can you chase one down?"

Bahtiyar smiled:

"You can see a thousand dreams and forget them all. But this one … But this one you would chase to the ends of the earth."

The shepherd thought for a moment and then said:

"Will you sell me your dream? I will pay you well for it."

Bahtiyar hesitated, then agreed:

"You are young and strong. Maybe you will find it quicker than I would."

He shared his dream, and in exchange, the shepherd gave Bahtiyar his entire flock: the dog, the donkey, the tent, and everything else. They even swapped names. The shepherd became Bahtiyar, and the old man took the name Malek-Mammad.

They parted ways. The new Bahtiyar went off into the world, and the older man, now Malek-Mammad, returned home, driving the flock before him. When he reached his village, his wife came running out, scolding him:

"Old man! Whose sheep are these? Aren't you ashamed? The neighbors will laugh, saying, 'Look, Bahtiyar has become a shepherd in his old age!'"

"Do not yell, woman," he said. "These sheep are mine. I traded my dream for them, and my name is no longer Bahtiyar. Now I am Malek-Mammad."

His wife stood there, stunned.

"Maybe he isn't my husband?" she wondered.

But the man said:

"Woman, you are losing your wits! it is me! I traded my dream, and my name too! I used to be poor, Bahtiyar. Now I am rich, Malek-Mammad."

Eventually, his wife came to understand, and they began living in wealth and comfort.

The New Bahtiyar

The new Bahtiyar, no longer the shepherd he once was, wandered through valleys and over mountains until he reached a walled city. It was already late, and the gates were closed. The guards refused to let him in, no matter how much he pleaded. So Bahtiyar had no choice but to sleep outside, under the open sky. Used to rough living, he curled up on the ground, pulled his coat tight around him, and drifted into a deep sleep.

In the middle of the night, he heard a voice calling:

"Bahtiyar! Bahtiyar! Wake up, Bahtiyar!"

Startled, he sat up, looking to the right, left, ahead, and up. He saw a shadowy figure standing atop the city wall, whispering urgently:

"Bahtiyar, hurry! Dawn is near. Grab the bag and follow me."

Bahtiyar was confused. "How did this stranger know my name?"

But he decided to trust fate. He grabbed the heavy bag waiting near the wall and moved closer. Suddenly, the gates creaked open, and a cloaked figure led two horses.

"Quick!" the stranger said. "Tie the bag to the saddle and mount up. We must be gone before anyone notices."

Bahtiyar swung into the saddle and rode off into the darkness without asking questions. They galloped all night without stopping. At sunrise, Bahtiyar finally saw who was riding beside him: A young woman so beautiful that he nearly fell off his horse from shock.

The young woman looked at him in surprise, too.

"Who are you?" she asked. "And what's your name?"

Bahtiyar smiled and said, "Hanum, did not you call for me yourself last night? I am Bahtiyar."

The girl gasped.

"You are Bahtiyar? Oh, no. I wasn't calling you! I was calling someone else."

She explained:

"I'm Zarniyar, the daughter of the great Shah of this land. I was supposed to run away with another Bahtiyar, the son of the Vizir, because my father wanted to marry me off to someone I did not love. But somehow fate sent you instead," she explained with a sigh. "Well, it must be destiny. There's no time to waste, we must leave my father's kingdom quickly!"

They spurred their horses and galloped hard, the wind howling around them. By nightfall, they reached another kingdom. They bought a beautiful house with gardens and fountains using the gold from the mysterious bag.

Bahtiyar shed his shepherd's clothes and dressed like a nobleman. He looked so handsome that no one could have guessed his humble beginnings. He and Zarniyar were married and lived happily together.

Though the dream Bahtiyar had bought had not yet come true, it seemed life had rewarded him with wealth, love, and happiness beyond anything he had imagined. But happiness, like a bird, often flies away when you least expect it.

The Jealous Shah

One day, Bahtiyar decided he needed a proper shave. But he did not want just any barber; he wanted the royal barber, who shaved the Shah himself. The royal barber came to Bahtiyar's house, but while wandering through the halls, he saw Zarniyar. One look at her beauty and the barber nearly dropped his tools.

He rushed back to the palace, his heart pounding. He burst into the Shah's chambers and cried out:

"Master of the World! How can you sit here alone while such beauty lives within your kingdom?"

The Shah frowned. "What are you talking about?" he growled. The barber described Zarniyar's beauty so vividly that the Shah's heart caught fire with jealousy and desire. Though he had never seen her, he decided immediately that he must be with her instead of Bahtiyar. He summoned his Vizir.

"Help me!" said the Shah. "I must see this woman."

The Vizir, sly as ever, smiled and said:

"Simple, O Ruler of the World. Invite yourself to Bahtiyar's home as a guest. Arrive early, before they expect you, and you will surely catch a glimpse of her."

The Shah clapped his hands in delight. He immediately sent a message to Bahtiyar stating that he would visit him tomorrow at noon.

When Bahtiyar received the message, he felt a deep sense of dread. He came home with heavy steps and his face clouded with worry. Zarniyar noticed right away.

"Light of my eyes, what troubles you?" she asked.

Bahtiyar told her everything. The clever Zarniyar only smiled.

"Do not worry," she said. "We'll welcome the Shah properly. Prepare a feast. Treat him like any other guest. Do not let fear show on your face."

The next morning, they cooked and cleaned, preparing a grand meal. But the Shah, following the Vizir's wicked plan, arrived an hour early. He burst through the door, and there stood Zarniyar, graceful and composed.

The Shah stared at her and felt like an arrow had struck him straight through the heart. He staggered and fainted on the spot. The Vizir rushed to revive him. Finally, the Shah sat up, his heart burning with an even greater desire.

That night, the Shah lay in bed, consumed by thoughts of Zarniyar. He called his Vizir again.

"I must marry her!" he cried. "But how can we get rid of Bahtiyar?"

The Vizir thought for a while and said:

"Send him on an impossible quest. Tell him to fetch heavenly apples, the kind that cure all illnesses. If he fails, you can have him executed."

The Shah loved this wicked idea. The next morning, he summoned Bahtiyar and said:

"My friend, I am very sick. The only thing that can save me is a heavenly apple. You have forty days to find one or face death."

The Journey for the Heavenly Apples

Bahtiyar returned home, his heart heavy. Zarniyar, seeing his sadness, asked what had happened. When he told her, she smiled calmly.

"Do not fear," she said. "Take this ring. Travel east for three days and three nights. You will reach the Land of the Deevs — mighty giants draped in shadow and fur, with horns that spiral like storm winds, voices that echo like thunder across the peaks, and strength great enough to crumble stone. Show them the ring, and they will serve you."

Bahtiyar kissed her hand, tucked the ring safely away, and set out immediately. He traveled through rocky valleys, wild rivers, and unknown lands. At last, on the morning of the fourth day, he reached the land of the Deevs. They rushed at him, roaring, but they fell to their knees when they saw the ring.

"What do you wish, Master?" they asked.

Bahtiyar said:

"I need heavenly apples."

One of the Deevs lifted him onto his back and soared into the sky, flying high over mountains and seas. The Deev carried Bahtiyar through clouds and winds until they finally landed beside a crystal-clear river shaded by an ancient Chinar tree.

"Hide behind the tree," the Deev whispered.

"Soon, three dove-sisters will arrive to bathe. They'll shed their feathers and reveal their human forms. Take the clothes of the youngest sister, but do not harm her. When you return her clothes, she will grant you any wish."

With that, the Deev disappeared into the mist. Bahtiyar hid behind the chinar tree and waited. Not long after, three beautiful doves swooped down from the sky. They fluttered to the riverbank, and each turned into a dazzling maiden in a blink. The oldest said:

"Let's bathe and cool off!"

But the middle sister hesitated.

"I had a bad dream," she said. "Maybe we shouldn't swim today."

The youngest laughed and twirled.

"We've flown so far, we deserve a swim!"

They tossed off their feathered cloaks and leaped into the water. Quick as a flash, Bahtiyar crept from behind the tree, snatched the youngest sister's cloak, and hid again. When the sisters finished bathing, two of them transformed easily into doves and flew away. But the youngest searched and searched, calling out in distress:

"My cloak! My cloak! I cannot leave without it!"

Then the oldest sister shouted into the trees:

"Whoever took our sister's robe, show yourself! Return it, we swear by the Shah's crown, and we will grant any wish!"

Bahtiyar stepped out and said:

"I seek heavenly apples. Bring them to me, and I will give back your cloak."

The youngest sister looked at him with bright, clever eyes and nodded.

In a flash, she leaped into the sky. Within an hour, she returned, carrying a branch heavy with golden apples. Bahtiyar carefully returned her feathered cloak. The sister smiled warmly before taking off into the sky. Bahtiyar held the branch of heavenly apples tightly. He slipped the magic ring onto his finger, and instantly, the Deev reappeared.

"Climb on," said the Deev.

Bahtiyar climbed onto the mighty creature's back, and they soared through the skies once again. After another three days and nights of flying, the Deev set him gently back on the road near his city gates. Bahtiyar thanked him sincerely and hurried straight to the palace, carrying the branch of apples.

The Shah, seeing Bahtiyar alive and holding the precious fruits, nearly fainted from shock.

"Oh, heavens above! You brought them back!" he cried out, forcing a smile.

He praised Bahtiyar with sweet words, but in his heart, he boiled with rage:

"This man is harder to get rid of than a rock in my shoe!"

Still, the Shah had no choice but to reward Bahtiyar with gold and riches, at least for now.

The Quest for the Rose of Gulistan

The Shah, seething with anger but hiding it behind a fake smile, called his Vizir again.

"What do we do now?" he hissed.

"This Bahtiyar … you send him anywhere, and he still comes back alive!"

The Vizir thought long and hard. Then, he snapped his fingers.

"I have it, Your Majesty! Tell Bahtiyar to bring you a rose from the Garden of Gulistan. That garden is hidden beyond mountains and deserts. No one knows the way. He will never return!"

The Shah grinned wickedly. Without wasting a moment, he summoned Bahtiyar.

"Dear friend," he said, sweet as honey, "you are the only one brave enough for this task. Bring me a rose from the Garden of Gulistan. You have forty days."

Bahtiyar bowed deeply but said nothing. He went home heavy-hearted. When he arrived, his wife, Zarniyar, immediately saw the sadness in his eyes.

"What is it, my love?" she asked.

"Why are you so troubled again?"

Bahtiyar told her everything.

Zarniyar just laughed lightly and said:

"Is that all? Do not worry! There's a way."

She whispered a secret magic verse into his ear.

"Memorize these words. Close your eyes and say them aloud. When you open your eyes again, you will find yourself in the Garden of Gulistan. Just keep in mind that there will be many beautiful girls, daughters of Peri kings, magical rulers from the fairy world. One among them shines brighter than all: Gullu Hanum. Do not look at her too long, and do not forget why you came."

Bahtiyar nodded, determined. He walked to the city gates, closed his eyes, and spoke the magic verse. The ground trembled under him, the winds swirled, and when he opened his eyes, he stood in a garden more beautiful than anything he could have imagined.

The Garden of Gulistan was alive with color and music. Roses bloomed in every shade, their perfume sweeter than dreams. Waterfalls glittered like jewels, and birds sang from crystal trees. Among the flowers, forty dazzling Peri girls danced, laughing and spinning like silver ribbons in the sun. Among them all, it was Gullu-Hanum whose beauty outshone the rest like the moon among stars. Her smile was so radiant that real roses fell from her lips when she laughed, covering the ground in a carpet of petals.

Bahtiyar tried to look away, but he couldn't. His heart raced. He forgot about the Shah. He forgot about the rose. He forgot everything as he became lost in Gullu Hanum's beauty.

Meanwhile, back at home, Zarniyar waited. She waited one day… two days… ten days… thirty-nine days. On the fortieth day, her heart ached with worry.

"Surely, the Peri princess has enchanted him," she thought.

Zarniyar closed her eyes without hesitation, spoke the magic verse, and flew to Gulistan herself. She arrived at the garden and saw exactly what she feared. Bahtiyar stood frozen, staring at the laughing Gullu hanum, lost in a dream. The other Peri girls giggled and danced, not noticing the newcomer. Quick as a blink, Zarniyar turned herself into a dove, and with a flap of her wings, turned Bahtiyar into a dove too. Together, they flew high into the sky, away from the garden.

When they landed safely back home, Zarniyar and Bahtiyar returned to their proper forms. Bahtiyar blinked, confused. Then he remembered everything: the quest, the Shah, the rose!

He gasped: "There's no time! I must bring the rose before the sun sets!"

But Zarniyar only smiled.

"Look," she said and pointed.

A perfect rose from Gulistan lay on their table, the treasure he had forgotten.

"Take it, and hurry!" she said.

Bahtiyar grabbed the rose and ran to the palace just before sunset. When the Shah saw Bahtiyar alive, and holding the impossible rose, he nearly fainted.

"Unbelievable…" he muttered through gritted teeth.

But he had no choice. He praised Bahtiyar again and showered him with gold. Yet deep in his heart, the Shah swore:

"This man must be destroyed!"

The Final Challenge

The Shah was boiling with rage. He stormed into his throne room, pacing back and forth. Then he screamed for his Vizir.

"Enough!" roared the Shah. "This time, Bahtiyar will not escape!"

The sly Vizir thought for a long time, rubbing his beard. Then he said:

"Command Bahtiyar should go to the Other World to visit your father and mother and bring back news of them. No man can return from such a journey!"

The Shah clapped his hands in delight.

"Brilliant!" he shouted.

At once, he summoned Bahtiyar. When Bahtiyar arrived, the Shah greeted him with a fake smile.

"My dear friend," he said smoothly, "I have another small favor to ask. Journey to the Afterlife and find out how my parents are doing. Bring back their news. You have forty days. If you fail, you know the price."

Bahtiyar bowed low but said nothing. He left the palace with a heart full of worry.

As soon as Bahtiyar walked through the door, Zarniyar could see something was wrong.

"My love," she said softly, "what has happened?"

Bahtiyar told her everything. Zarniyar smiled calmly.

"Do not worry," she said. "I know how to save you."

She whispered her plan into his ear:

"Go back to the Shah. Tell him you need a giant bonfire built in the main square, a mountain of wood soaked in oil. You will climb to the top. When the fire is lit, thick black smoke will rise, and I will transform you into a small stick and carry you away as a dove. The fire will hide everything."

Bahtiyar's heart lifted with hope. He kissed Zarniyar's hands and rushed back to the palace. Bahtiyar stood before the Shah and said:

"O mighty Shah, build me a fire so high it touches the sky! Pour oil over it so it burns hotter than the sun. I will climb to the very top, and the smoke will carry me to your parents."

The Shah clapped his hands in glee. "Let the fire be prepared immediately," he ordered.

Hundreds of servants hauled wood and barrels of oil into the square. A mountain of firewood rose higher than any house. The people gathered, whispering in amazement.

At sunrise, Bahtiyar climbed to the very top of the pile. He waved to the crowd below.

"Light it!" he cried.

The Shah, with his hand, threw the first torch into the darkness. The fire roared to life, crackling and hissing. Smoke billowed upward, covering Bahtiyar from sight. But hidden in the smoke, Zarniyar transformed herself into a dove, turned Bahtiyar into a tiny stick, and gripping him gently in her beak, flew safely away. The Shah, his Vizir, and all their men tossed wood into the flames all night, sure they had finally destroyed Bahtiyar.

They had no idea. At dawn on the fortieth day, Zarniyar woke Bahtiyar.

"It's time to finish this," she said.

She gave him three scrolls: one for the Shah, one for the Vizir, and one for the wicked barber who had first betrayed them. Bahtiyar carried the scrolls to the ashes of the great fire. He buried himself under the cold gray ashes, hiding from view.

Soon, the Shah and his Vizir came to the square. They began kicking through the ashes, pretending to "honor" Bahtiyar's sacrifice. But suddenly, the ashes stirred! Bahtiyar emerged from the ashes, scorched and soot-covered, but very much alive.

"Greetings, mighty Shah!" He cried cheerfully. "I saw your parents in the Afterlife! They send you their regards, and a little message."

He handed the scrolls to the Shah and his men. When they opened the scrolls, their faces turned red with shame. The message read:

"Shame on you! You sent your son-in-law to die instead of visiting your parents yourself! Come to us yourself if you dare!"

The people watching began to laugh and whisper among themselves. The Shah and his men were humiliated.

Seeing no escape, the Shah ordered a great fire built again, but this time for himself, the Vizir, and the barber. They climbed the wood pile, and the flames carried them away, this time for good.

The people rejoiced. They turned to Bahtiyar and cried:

"We have waited long for someone like you. Step into the royal palace, your rightful place. You are the Shah we have long hoped for."

And so Bahtiyar became Shah. He ruled wisely and kindly, with Zarniyar by his side, the bravest and cleverest woman. Their palace was filled with light and laughter.

As for the old dream, Bahtiyar searched for it, and though he never found it exactly as he imagined, he saw something far greater. Sometimes, the true treasures are not the ones we chase, but the ones we earn through courage and kindness.

The Tale of the Stingy Julfa and Clever

Teymur

ong ago, in a faraway town, there lived a man named Julfa. He was known not just for his shiny bald head, but even more for being the stingiest man anyone had ever met. Not a single coin ever left his hand for those in need, not even a crumb of bread for the hungry. His wife, Fatima, was his opposite; kind, open hearted, and loved by everyone who knew her.

In that same town lived a boy named Teymur. He had lost both of his parents and was left on his own. Before her marriage, Fatima had also been orphaned. It was Teymur's father, a man known for his generosity, who had taken her in and raised her as his daughter.

When Fatima came of age, Julfa married her. Teymur's father gave her a proper dowry and blessed their union. Not long after, Teymur lost both his father and mother. Alone in the world, he often visited Fatima, who remained the closest person to his family.

Fatima would always try to help him with a warm meal or a change of clothes, but Julfa hated it. Every time Teymur appeared, Julfa would scowl and mutter under his breath.

One day, driven by hunger, Teymur came to their door. Fatima saw him and tried to think of a way to feed him without upsetting her husband.

"Teymur," she said gently, "come in and watch the baby while I step out. I will feed you when I return."

But Julfa overheard and interrupted her. "No need," he growled. "Put the baby in the cradle, tie one end of a rope to the cradle and the other to my left hand. As I work, my arm swings. The cradle will rock."

Fatima did as she was told, holding back her frustration.

She tried again. "There's some grain on the roof. Teymur can guard it from the birds and chickens."

Julfa barked again: "Bring a long pole, tie one end to my right hand, and stick the other through the chimney. My hand moves while I work. The pole will wave and scare them off."

Calm as ever, Fatima obeyed. But deep down, she wasn't done yet.

"We have sour milk," she said. "Teymur can churn it into butter."

"Strap the churn to my back," said Julfa. "My spine bends and straightens when I weave. It'll churn on its own."

"The fireplace is cracked," she said next. "Teymur can mix clay and fix it."

"Pour sand and water in a tub at my feet. As I work, my steps will mix the clay."

Each attempt was met with a new command, reducing human kindness to mechanical movement.

Realizing she was out of options, Fatima looked helplessly at Teymur. He smiled weakly and walked away.

Wandering the streets, he muttered to himself, "If only fate turned Julfa into the one in need, I would teach him a lesson he wouldn't forget."

Then, near the city gate, he saw a big crowd gathering.

"What's going on?" he asked a neighbor.

"The Shah lost a jewel from his royal ring. He has promised a reward: gold equal to the finder's weight."

People were scouring the road. Teymur joined in. As others gave up, he decided to search crosswise instead of lengthwise, and soon, a flash caught his eye. There it was, the missing jewel, right beneath his feet.

He ran to the palace gates.

"Stop there. Where are you going, young men?" a guard sneered.

"Hurry. Let me through. I found the Shah's jewel."

"Let me see it."

"No, I will not. It belongs to the Great Shah."

"Give it to me. I will reward you."

"No, I will take it to him myself."

"Then I will not let you through this gate."

"Open the gate, or I will raise my voice until the Great Shah hears."

The guard gave in. Another stopped him at the inner gate, but Teymur was undeterred. He insisted on seeing the Shah, brushing past bribes and threats. At last, he was brought before the Vizir.

"What business do you have?"

"With all due respect, my business is not with you, Vizir. It is with the Shah."

Impressed by his resolve, the Vizir brought him forward.

"Your Majesty," said Teymur, bowing, "I found your lost jewel."

The Shah was delighted. "Thank you, young men. You may go now."

"Wait," said Teymur in disbelief. "You issued a decree. The finder would be rewarded with his weight in gold. Where is the gold?"

The Shah appeared surprised and said, "Perhaps my announcer exaggerated the reward... But tell me, what do you want in return?"

Teymur stepped forward, bowed respectfully, and replied,

"Oh, Most Kind Shah, I do not want your gold. But I would be honored if you wrote a royal order for me."

"What kind of order?" the Shah asked, narrowing his eyes with curiosity.

Teymur stood tall and answered clearly,

"An order stating that from this day on, every bald man in the city must pay me a one-time tax of 100 silver coins, as compensation for finding the Shah's missing jewel."

The Shah chuckled. "Fine. I am not bald."

"Also add, every man named Julfa."

"Alright."

"And everyone whose wife is named Fatima.

"Very well."

"And every donkey owner."

"Sure."

"And every man from the village of Serhan-Bayli."

"Go on."

"And anyone who breaks the decree must pay 1,000 silver coins."

"Done."

"Lastly, add that anyone who witnesses a violation and does nothing? They must pay 1,000 silver coins as well."

With a raised eyebrow, the Shah signed the decree and sealed it. Teymur bowed and said, "I will be right back in about an hour."

One hour later, he was back.

"Someone has broken your decree and now owes me 1,000 coins."

"Who dares? Bring him here!"

The Shah summoned his executioners, and when they arrived, he turned to Teymur and asked: "Where is the one who broke my royal decree?"

Teymur replied calmly

"May blessings be upon the Great Shah. Did you not issue a decree stating that whoever breaks your decree must pay a fine of 1,000 silver coins?"

"Yes, I did," confirmed the Shah.

"Then why haven't you given me a single coin? You are the first to break your decree by not rewarding me when I found your jewel. You can pay me the original reward, pay me a fine, or order your head to be cut off."

Hearing this, the Shah flew into a rage.

"You fool! Are you mocking me?! I will have you…"

"May blessings be upon the Shah," interrupted Teymur. "You may order me beaten, even beheaded. But know that dozens of others have copies of this decree," said Teymur. "If something happens to me, people will know the truth."

Realizing he had no way to avoid a public scandal and potential for trouble, the Shah decided to pay a fine.

"Your Vizir saw this and said nothing. That is also 1,000 silver coins," continued Teymur.

The Vizir handed over the money, muttering complaints under his breath.

Teymur bowed respectfully and left the palace for Julfa's house. Upon arriving, he called out to Julfa, unrolled the Shah's decree bearing all the royal seals, and asked: "Julfa, since you are bald, you fall under the new decree signed by the Great Shah. And by that order, you owe me a fine of 100 silver coins."

"What are you talking about?"

"And since your name is Julfa. That is another 100 coins."

"Fatima! Come deal with your brother!"

"So, your wife's name is Fatima? Another 100 coins."

"You have a donkey? Another 100 coins."

"You are from Serhan-Bayli? Another 100."

"Refuse, and you will be fined 1,000 for breaking the Great Shah's decree."

Julfa read the decree and, with shaking hands, handed over the silver coins.

"And since you watched the law being broken without doing anything. That is another 1,000."

Julfa, speechless and with a hand over his heart, paid once again.

"Let that be your lesson," said Teymur.

Fatima smiled. "Looks like generosity runs in the family after all."

Julfa, once the stingiest man in town, slowly changed his ways. He began to share, to speak kindly, and to open his door to those in need. As for Teymur, he grew into a respected leader known for his wisdom, courage, and profound commitment to justice.

Greed may deceive the heart with money, but it depletes the true wealth of loving family and friends. Ultimately, karma ensures that even the stingy must pay the price.

The Lazy Man and the Road to Fortune

Long ago, in a small village nestled between rocky ridges and sun-dried fields, there lived a man named Sheydulla. He was well-known around the region for his laziness.

All day long, his wife and children worked, constantly feeling hungry. Sheydulla, on the other hand, spent his days lying under the shade of their crumbling mud-brick house, daydreaming of riches.

"Do not worry," he would tell his wife, flashing a lazy grin. "We may be poor now, but soon we'll get rich!"

"Rich?" she cried. "How can we be rich when you won't lift a finger? The goats are starving, our roof is leaking, and the children do not have shoes to put on their bare feet!"

"Just wait," Sheydulla yawned. "One day, it will all change."

But no change ever came. Finally, his wife could hold out no longer. "We're starving, Sheydulla! Do something, or we are all doomed."

So, at last, Sheydulla stood up, stretched like a cat, and announced he decided to seek the wisdom of the great sage who lived beyond the mountains. "He will tell me how to become rich without breaking my back."

He set off on the journey, walking three days and three nights. On the fourth morning, a thin gray wolf stepped onto the path.

"Where are you heading, lazy man?"

"I am going to the wise sage," Sheydulla replied. "I need to ask him how to become wealthy without work."

The wolf groaned. "Could you ask him something for me while you there? I've had a terrible stomachache for three years. I've been suffering from it day and night. If the sage knows the cure, I beg him to tell me."

"Sure," said Sheydulla as he continued his way.

Three more days and nights passed, and he arrived at a peaceful spring where a beautiful apple tree stood.

"Where are you going, kind traveler?" asked the tree.

"To seek fortune from the wise sage," said Sheydulla.

"Could you please ask him something for me?" the tree questioned. "Each spring I blossom with joy, but all my flowers fall before they bear fruit. What is wrong with me?"

"Sure, I will ask," Sheydulla promised.

He journeyed again for three days and nights until he reached a vast, still lake. A large fish poked her head from the water.

"Traveler," she called, "where are you going?"

"To see the sage," he answered.

"Please," begged the fish, "could you ask him why I have a thorn in my throat? It has been causing me pain for seven years. If it is removed, I could live in peace."

Sheydulla agreed and continued. Finally, after twelve days of walking, he entered a rose-filled grove. Beneath one bush sat an old man with a snow-white beard.

"You've come a long way, Sheydulla," said the sage.

Sheydulla gasped. "How do you know my name?"

"Names travel faster than feet," said the sage with a wink. "Now, why are you here?"

Sheydulla expressed his desire to become rich without working. He then recounted the requests made by the wolf, the apple tree, and the fish.

The sage listened patiently and then said:

"The fish has a precious gemstone stuck in her throat. Whoever removes it will cure her and gain wealth beyond imagining.

Beneath the apple tree, a pot of silver is buried. If dug up, its blossoms will produce sweet fruit.

"And the wolf? He can only be healed by devouring the first lazy man he meets."

Sheydulla blinked. "And what about me?"

The sage smiled. "Your answer has already been given. Now, go with peace."

Overjoyed, Sheydulla turned back home. He soon reached the lake, where the fish met him eagerly.

"Did the sage give an answer?"

"Yes," said Sheydulla. "A jewel lies in your throat. Remove it, and you will be healed."

"Please help me to remove it!" the fish begged. "And take the treasure for yourself."

But Sheydulla shrugged. "Why would I do that? The whole point is I do not want to work. Besides, the sage said I will be rich anyway."

He left the fish in pain and moved on.

The apple tree rustled in joy as he approached. "What did the sage say?"

"Dig beneath your roots, and you will find silver. That will cure your blossoms."

"Please help me, start to dig! The silver would be yours too!"

But Sheydulla shook his head. "That is too much work. My riches are coming without using a shovel."

At last, he met the wolf.

"Well? What did the sage say?"

"He said the first lazy man you find is your cure. Eat him, and your pain will vanish."

The wolf looked Sheydulla up and down and said, "Well, I do not have to search any longer."

With a snap of his jaws, he swallowed Sheydulla.

So, the man who dreamed of wealth without lifting a finger was swallowed by the very answer he carried, a fitting end for someone who hoped but never acted.

The tale of Sheydulla the Lazy reminds the young and old that dreams alone do not change anything. It's wisdom, effort, and action that are the keys to changing one's destiny.

The Gardener and the Magic Crown

Long ago, in the valley of the Lower Caucasus mountains, in a sunny village filled with birdsong and the smell of jasmine, there lived an old gardener named Rustam Baba.

Rustam Baba had an extraordinary garden filled with pomegranate, fig, peach, and mulberry trees, alongside beautiful roses, tulips, and jasmine. Nightingales sang like flutes in this enchanting setting. Children played in the shade. Bees buzzed lazily in the warm air.

Word of this garden spread far, and one day, the news of this magical garden reached the ears of the Shah, the ruler of the land, who lived in the castle overlooking the valley. He sat on his golden throne, listening to the Vizir.

"Such a beautiful garden is worthy only of a Shah," said the Shah, twirling his mustache. "I must have it."

"Of course, Your Majesty," the Vizir agreed at once, "I will take care of it immediately."

That very same day, the Vizir sent Shah's soldiers with orders down to the valley to the beautiful garden. The soldier read the Shah's orders, which stated that the garden and the land on which it grew belonged to the Shah. The gardener must leave immediately.

Rustam Baba was shocked. "But this is my life," he cried

"I grew every fruit with these hands. How will I feed my family?"

"That is not our concern. We follow the order of the Shah," said the soldiers. "He gives nothing back."

And just like that, Rustam Baba was thrown out of his garden. He returned home in sorrow and sat on the floor, silent. His wife, Fatima, brought him tea.

"What's wrong, Rustam? What are you thinking about?" she asked.

"The Shah…. The Shah stole our garden," he sighed.

"Stole?! What do you mean? How is that possible? Did we owe him anything?"

"No. Shah heard of its beauty and decided to take it. He sent soldiers claiming that everything in the kingdom belonged to him, including the garden, and kicked me out. Fatima slammed down the teacup in disbelief.

"Did he give you anything in return?" she asked.

"What are you talking about? Shah always takes from those who cannot defend themselves or have no one to defend on their behalf."

"Then he is not a legitimate ruler. He is a thief in a crown!"

That last word strutted Rustam Baba. He looked at Fatima, and his facial expression changed. He had a sparkle in his eye.

"I have an idea," he whispered. "I will make him a crown that suits him best. "

"What?" Fatima said, surprised by the sudden change in Rustam's mood.

"The Shah loves compliments and flattery more than water in summer. I will make him believe in something," he paused "something invisible, yet grand. Something as fictitious as its greatness."

"You mean trick him?" Fatima gasped.

"Yes," said Rustam Baba. "He took our garden with greed. I will use his greed to teach him a lesson."

The next day, he changed his clothes, packed old bits of iron into a cloth sack, tied on his turban, and marched uphill toward the Shah's palace. When he reached the gates, he told the guards:

"Peace upon you, mighty guards of the Shah. I am a world-famous master jewel craftsman. I bring a gift for the Shah!"

The guard announced his presence, and the Shah welcomed him inside the palace.

"May your days be bright, o mighty Shah," said Rustam Baba.

"I am here to make you an offer. I can create the world's most magical crown that would make your enemies jealous. A magical crown that only your friends can see, but your enemies would see nothing!"

The Shah's eyes lit up like lanterns.

"If you make this crown, I will give you whatever you ask!"

"Most certainly, I only need a half pound of gold and twenty different gems, and I can complete the magical crown in forty days", said the gardener.

The Shah clapped his hands and shouted at the Vizir. "Give him what he needs!" He turned to Rustam Baba. "Return in forty days, or I will take your head!"

Rustam Baba collected the gold and returned home. On his way home, he bought food and clothes for his family and then waited.

As days pass, Fatima worries.

"The days are passing! What will you do?"

"Do not worry, Fatima," he smiled. "I have already made the crown. it is in their minds."

On the fortieth day, on a beautiful morning, Rustam Baba walked the streets and announced to everyone:

"Friends, neighbors, gather 'round! Meet me in the castle square, I've got something dazzling to show you: the Shah's brand-new crown!"

The people came in crowds. The Shah sat on a tall throne, surrounded by his Vizir, advisors, generals, and guards. Drums rolled.

Rustam Baba bowed and spoke loudly:

"Behold! A crown that only true friends of the Shah can see. Enemies will see nothing!"

He reached into his empty sack, waved his bare hands, and placed absolutely nothing on the Shah's head. The crowd froze in silence.

The Vizir was the first to run towards Shah and stated

"Amazing! The crown shines like a thousand stars!"

The advisor blinked, saw nothing, but feared being called a traitor.

"Truly, it glows brighter than the moon!"

Even the general bowed and declared:

"This crown is so bright that we do not need sunlight anymore!"

The crowd clapped and cheered, though none saw a thing. Some were scared to speak, but others just copied the rest.

The Shah, feeling nothing, touched his head and cried, "Bring me a mirror!"

When he looked at the mirror, he saw nothing. He looked at the gardener with mixed emotions, ready to shout at the guards but stopped. He thought that if he said he saw nothing, he would be ridiculed by the crowd.

He stood up and boomed:

"Let all loyal subjects shower the craftsman with gifts!"

Jewels, rugs, and gold coins, were all poured at Rustam Baba's feet.

The Shah pulled Rustam Baba aside when the celebration ended, and the crowd was gone.

"Old man… what have you done? You have not just fooled me - you fooled the entire court!"

"Your Majesty," said Rustam Baba, bowing deeply. "I am the old man whose garden you took. Without it, I cannot feed my family. I meant no disrespect, but that was my defense. I do not have or want to raise a weapon against you. I used my wisdom instead."

The Shah was silent. Then he asked:

"What if I punish you now?"

"Then all your people will say: 'Look at the Shah. He punishes the man who gave him a crown.'"

The Shah paused. He realized he would lose all respect if he were to punish the old man. He laughed.

"You are braver than a soldier and sharper than my Vizir. Go home in peace."

Rustam Baba returned to his family with treasure bags and his head held high. He never got his garden, but he planted a new one. With the help of his kids and Fatima, they planted many fruit trees and flowers together. Soon, the new flowers were blooming, the trees grew tall and produced fruit, bees buzzed, nightingales sang like flutes, and children played beneath the shade. Every flower whispered a secret:

Those blinded by power are no match for the wisdom of the humble.

How Jirtan Outsmarted the Giant Deev

ong ago, in the land of fire and wind, a woman lived with her son, so small that everyone called him Jirtan, which means "the Little One." Despite his small size, Jirtan was a very active child and always tried to help his mother in any way he could.

One day, he saw the neighborhood boys gathering firewood in the forest.

"Mama," said Jirtan, "can I go with them?" he pointed out to the boys.

His mother looked at him with concern. "You are too small, my dear. You cannot even lift a twig!"

"But the other boys will help me," Jirtan said with a smile.

Jirtan's mother wasn't about to let her tiny son head into the forest without making sure he was safe. She called over the older neighborhood boys, handed each of them a piece of flatbread wrapped around a slice of cheese, and looked at them firmly.

"Boys," she said, "my Jirtan may be small, but he is eager to help. I am trusting you do not let him wander off or get lost in the woods."

The boys nodded, understanding the responsibility they were given. With food in hand and Jirtan tagging along, they set off toward the trees.

The children followed the path into the forest, chatting and laughing as they began gathering firewood. Even little Jirtan joined in, eager to help. He reached for branches with all his might, but most were too big or heavy for him to carry. Still, he did not give up. He tugged and dragged what he could, determined to do his part.

"Let's help Jirtan," the boys said. They tied together a small bundle of firewood for him to carry.

However, when it was time to go home, Jirtan found himself unable to lift his bundle.

"I cannot move it! Can someone help me, please?" he called out.

The boys hurried back and, with cheerful teasing, helped Jirtan lift his bundle onto his shoulders. But as they laughed and talked, they did not notice how quickly the sun had slipped away behind the trees. By the time they looked around, night had fallen, and the forest paths were gone. They were lost. The boys looked around, but they couldn't find the path home, and a ripple of panic began to set in. From one direction, they heard the distant barking of dogs echoing through the trees. From the other, they spotted a faint glow of firelight flickering far away.

"Which way, Jirtan?" the older boys asked.

Jirtan thought for a moment. "Let's not go where the dogs are, because it could be dangerous. That light might be a house. Let's head there."

So, they followed the dim glow, hoping it would lead them to safety. They walked toward the light. The oldest boy carried Jirtan on his back so he wouldn't fall behind.

Eventually, they reached a house by the river with a heavy wooden door that creaked in the wind. It looked old and quiet. The kids knocked on the door and called out, "Please let us stay the night!"

Suddenly, the door creaked open, and a monstrous giant Deev stood in the doorway. His arms were long, and his body was covered in coarse fur, dark as storm clouds. Two big horns arched from the side of his head like crescent moons, and beneath them shone a pair of wide, gleeful eyes above a crooked nose that gave him a fearsome appearance. When he grinned, his jagged teeth glimmered in the dim light, and he stared at the children with a hungry, wicked gleam.

When the Deev saw how frightened the children looked, he quickly changed his tone and tried to sound friendly.

"Come in, little ones," he said with a smile that did not quite reach his eyes. "Stay the night, and I will show you the way home in the morning."

But behind this act of kindness, he was thinking about dinner, and the children were on the menu. He gave them food and tucked them into the guest bed. Then he sat by the fire, waiting for them to fall asleep.

"Who's asleep, and who's still awake?" the Deev whispered in the dark.

"I'm still awake," said Jirtan, his voice calm.

"Why aren't you sleeping?" the Deev asked, leaning closer.

"Because every night, my mama makes me eggs before bed, and you didn't!"

Grumbling under his breath, the Deev stomped off to the kitchen and fried some eggs. Jirtan ate them and curled up again under his blanket.

The Deev sat by the fire once more, patiently waiting for Jirtan to fall asleep. A few minutes passed.

"Who's asleep, and who's still awake?" the Deev whispered in the dark.

"I'm still awake," said Jirtan, his voice calm.

"Why aren't you sleeping?" the Deev asked, leaning closer.

"Because every night, my mama brings me river water in a basket before I sleep!"

The Deev sighed and muttered to himself. Then he rummaged around and found an old woven basket. "If that is what the little one wants…" he grumbled.

He stomped down to the river and tried to scoop up water, but the wooden basket was full of cracks, and the water streamed out between the slats before he could take a single step. Again and again, he tried, getting wetter and grumpier each time.

While the Deev was still down by the river, grumbling and splashing, Jirtan quietly woke the other boys.

"Shh! That Deev is planning to eat us," he whispered. "We have to get out of here, now!"

The boys nodded, wide-eyed. One by one, they tiptoed out of the house.

Down by the river, the Deev was too busy scooping water with his leaky basket to notice a thing.

Carefully, the boys crept past him in the shadows, holding their breath. When they reached the river's edge, they helped each other across, splashing softly until all of them made it safely to the other side.

When the Deev finally looked up and saw the boys on the far side of the river, he roared,

"Hey! How did you get across?"

Jirtan cupped his hands around his mouth and called back,

"Oh, that is easy! We tied a big, heavy stone around our necks to help us float across and jumped into the river. Try it. It works great!"

The Deev found a heavy millstone, tied it around his neck, and leaped into the river. But the stone was too heavy for the Deev, who could not swim. It pulled him under, and he sank to the bottom of the river. That is how clever little Jirtan saved all his friends from the terrible Deev.

The boys followed the path through the forest, and just as the sun was rising, they finally found their way home.

Jirtan's mother had been waiting all night, eyes full of worry. When she saw him, she ran to him, scooped him into her arms, and hugged him tight. He told her everything that had happened in "the forest, the night, the scary Deev, and how he saved all the boys."

His mother listened with wide eyes, then wrapped her arms around him and said softly,

"My brave little hero… You may be small, but your heart is stronger than any giant."

With courage and wit, even the smallest can triumph over the mighty.

The Secret of Friendship

The Floating Chest

L ong ago, in a faraway land, there lived a mighty Shah who ruled with wisdom and strength. His family members were more precious than his entire kingdom, and that was his only son, Prince Malik. The young prince was kind-hearted, curious, and brave, admired by everyone in the land.

One bright morning, Malik went riding along the shores of the Caspian Sea. As he trotted along, he spotted two men by the water's edge. One of them was his stableman and a clever fellow named Kechal Mamed. Kechal, known for his sharp mind and quick wit, was a legendary figure in folk tales. But today, he was locked in a furious brawl with the stableman. They were shouting, shoving, and throwing fists.

Malik galloped over and jumped off his horse. "Stop! What is this fight about?" he demanded.

The two men separated, huffing and puffing. The stableman spoke first. "My prince, I saw a strange chest floating in the sea. I swam out and pulled it to shore. But just as I got it out, Kechal appeared and claimed he saw it first. He insists the chest is his."

Malik looked at them sternly. "You are both acting foolishly." He handed each man a silver coin and said, "Let this end your quarrel." Then, he took the mysterious chest, loaded it on his horse, and rode back toward the palace.

On the way, curiosity overpowered him. "What's inside this chest that sparked such a fight?" He decided to stop and opened it.

Inside was another, smaller, and older chest. He opened that one, too, and found a third box, this one no bigger than a jewelry case. Inside, it was a delicate scroll. Malik unrolled it and read the faded writing:

"He who seeks the secret of true friendship must find the Fortress of the Three Elders."

A Prince's Request

The scroll's words stirred something profound in Malik's heart. He rushed to the palace and found his father in the garden.

"My dear father," he said, "I want to ask for your blessing to take a journey. Something important got me curious, and I cannot rest until I find it."

The Shah frowned. "What is it, son?"

Malik hesitated. He did not want to sound foolish. But when the shah pressed him, Malik told him the whole story from the chest by the sea to the message hidden in the scroll.

When he finished, the Shah laughed. "My son do not let every scribble or mystery pull you away from home. The world is full of nonsense. Friendship is something you can learn right here. There's no need to chase shadows."

Malik pleaded, but the Shah was firm. "You are my only heir. I will not risk sending you into danger on a wild quest because of some mysterious scribbles."

Heartbroken, Malik retreated to a hidden chamber in the palace: the Room of Sorrows. The walls, floor, and ceiling were all black, and no light entered. People only entered this room to grieve. Malik dressed in black and stayed there for days, weeping.

The Shah grew worried. He sent guards to search the palace, and after days of searching, they found Malik in the dark room, pale and worn. The Shah and his Vizir came to see him.

"My son," the Shah said gently, "why this sorrow?"

Malik knelt before him. "I asked you to let me find the secret of true friendship, and you said no. Your decision pains me and it has left me hollow."

The Shah sighed. He offered his son riches, pleasures, and honors —
anything but the journey, but Malik only repeated: "Let me find the
secret of true friendship."

After much discussion, the Shah gave in. "Very well," he said. "You may
go on your journey, but with one condition. I will send one hundred
warriors to guard you."

That was the Vizir's plan. He whispered an alternative plan to Shah.
"Have the soldiers quietly leave him, one by one. When he is alone, he
will grow scared and come home."

The Shah agreed.

New Companion

Malik rode out the next morning, leading a shining column of soldiers.
Not long after they left the palace, they met Kechal Mamed on the road.

"Where are you headed, Prince Malik?" Mamed asked.

Malik smiled. "I'm seeking the Fortress of the Three Elders. According
to the scroll I found inside the chest, the secret of true friendship lies
there."

Kechal rubbed his chin. "That sounds like an adventure worth joining.
Wait here, I will tell my parents."

Soon, he returned with his saddlebags filled with barley bread his mother
had packed. Together, Malik and Kechal set off down the road.

As the days passed, the soldiers began to vanish, just as the Vizir had
planned. One by one, they disappeared until Malik and Kechal were
utterly alone.

Kechal grew anxious. "We're alone in the wild. What can we do without
protection or weapons?"

Malik frowned. "If you want to go home, go. But I am not turning back."

Kechal sighed. "No, my Prince. If this journey is meant for anyone, it is
for me. I am with you."

Their journey has just begun.

The Golden Fortress

They traveled far, through thick forests and deserts, across rivers and hills. One day, they reached a towering mountain. It took them three days to climb it, and when they reached the top and descended the other side, they gasped.

Below lay a valley like none they'd seen before. It was blanketed in flowers of every color imaginable, glowing like precious stones. Birds with feathers of turquoise and gold flitted through the trees, and deer grazed without fear. In the middle of the valley stood a castle made of gold and silver bricks. Its towers touched the clouds. A massive stone wall surrounded it, and just looking at it made their hearts race.

"This must be the Fortress of the Three Elders," Malik said in awe.

But Kechal frowned. "Hmm… it is too quiet. Too perfect."

As they approached the gate, the ground rumbled beneath them. A thunderous crash shook the air. Suddenly, enormous hands, disembodied and silent, emerged from nowhere. One hand lifted Malik from his horse; another grabbed Kechal. More hands took their horses by the reins and led them into a huge stable.

Inside the stable, the invisible hands fed and watered the horses. Then, they guided the travelers into the castle.

It was the most luxurious place Malik had ever seen. Rich tapestries, golden furniture, and diamond chandeliers made even the royal palace seem plain in comparison. But not a single person was in sight. The hands reappeared with towels and water for washing, then set a lavish table full of dishes neither Malik nor Kechal had seen before. The hypnotic aroma of food made their mouths water.

They ate and were shown to a chamber with beds as soft as clouds. Malik fell asleep instantly. Kechal, ever cautious, only pretended to sleep.

Well past midnight, the door creaked open. Three older men entered. All wore black robes and tall turbans. One held a book, another a staff, and the third had a curved sword with a black hilt.

The one with the sword scowled. "We should kill them. If they learn our secrets, we are doomed."

"No," said the one with the book. "The prince's father will come for revenge. And destiny still has plans for Kechal Mamed."

"Then what do we do?" the staff bearer asked.

"We help them," said the one with the book. "They've come a long way. Let them prove they're worthy."

Kechal jumped up and knelt before them. "Wise ones," he pleaded. "We only want to learn the meaning of true friendship. Please help us."

The elder with the book extended his hand. "At dawn, ride east. You will meet a fox, which is a witch in disguise. Do not speak to her. When you pass her, flip your horses' shoes backward to lose her trail."

"Then you will see a bird with feathers of every color. do not harm it. Feed it a little grain and move on."

"When you reach the sea, look for a black stone. This stone weighs 2,000 pounds, but do not worry. Say: ' O black stone, you fell from the sky, and the earth embraced you. Now, please help us.' Lift the stone to find magical reins. Throw one end of the reins into the sea, and a three-legged horse will emerge. Ride it across the water, as this horse lives in the sea and cannot walk on dry land. Once you reach the other side, remove the reins and release the horse. There, you will find another black stone. Repeat the same spell to lift this stone and leave the reins beneath it.

Afterward, you will discover iron shoes and a staff. Put them on and walk until they wear out. That will be where your path ends, and you will meet an old woman. Give her some coins, and she will show you the place you have been searching for."

The three elders vanished instantly, and Kechal rushed to wake Malik, who was sleeping soundly. When Malik woke up, he shouted angrily,

"Why did you wake me? I was having the most incredible dream! If you'd been in my place, you'd never want to wake up..."

But Kechal Mamed ignored his reaction and replied calmly,

"My prince, you are lucky you slept through it all. If only you knew how those old men frightened me."

"Old men? What are you talking about?" Malik asked, confused.

So Kechal told him everything he had seen and heard. Everything, except for one small detail.

He said, "When we see the bird, we must shoot it."

As the saying goes, there's no one trickier than Kechal. He thought, "what if we argue on the way? What if Malik, thinking he knows best, sends me away and reaches the place alone? Better he doesn't know everything."

After that, Kechal made Malik promise to follow his lead on the journey, regardless of the circumstances. They swore an oath of eternal friendship and sealed it with their blood.

The Witch at the Crossroads

At the first light of dawn, Malik and Kechal Mamed quietly slipped out of the castle gates. Their two horses, fully saddled, were waiting for them, held once again by the silent hands that had served them the night before.

They mounted and rode east as instructed. The morning was cool, and the birdsong echoed through the valley. After a few hours, they came upon a dusty clearing where seven narrow paths branched out like fingers from a palm. Sitting right in the middle of the crossroads was a fox. But it was no ordinary fox; its eyes glowed green, and its coat shimmered as if dusted with gold.

The fox stood up and, to their surprise, began to speak with the voice of an old woman. "Good morning, travelers," it said. "You've come far. Tell me, where you are headed? What is it you seek?"

Kechal whispered to Malik, "This is the witch. do not say a word."

Malik nodded. They nudged their horses forward, ignoring the fox's questions. The fox trotted beside them, pretending to stumble, begging for help, flattering them, even threatening them. But the two friends remained silent, riding steadily ahead.

Once they were a safe distance away and out of sight, they dismounted, took off the horses' shoes, and reattached them backward, just as the elder had advised.

"I hope that throws her off," said Malik.

"It will. I would bet my last slice of barley bread on it," said Kechal with a grin.

Back in the clearing, the fox-witch sniffed the dust, trying to follow their trail. But the reversed horseshoes led her in the wrong direction, and soon, she was gone.

The path ahead was long and quiet. By midday, they saw a bright fluttering speck the air. A tiny bird, no larger than a fist, flew down and landed on a low branch. Each feather gleamed with a thousand colors. It cocked its head and looked at them with curious eyes.

Malik reached for his bow.

"No, wait!" Kechal cried out. "Prince Malik, please forgive me for not telling you the truth earlier," he added quickly. "The wise man said we must feed the birds."

Malik slowly lowered his bow and looked at Kechal, then reached into his satchel. He crumbled a piece of barley bread and scattered it on the ground. The colorful bird fluttered down, pecked at the crumbs, and let out a high, sweet trill before soaring back into the sky.

Kechal smiled with relief. "Prince Malik, forgive me again for doubting you. We are in this together."

They continued until they reached the edge of the sea. The waves crashed against the rocks, and the wind carried the scent of salt and adventure. On the shore stood a large, black stone, just as the elder had described.

Malik stepped forward and placed his hand on the cold stone. He spoke the words: "O black stone, you fell from the sky, the earth held you, now, please help us."

The stone suddenly grew lighter. Malik lifted it easily and found a set of magical reins lying underneath. He picked them up and threw one end into the sea.

The ocean roared. A column of water rose from the depths, and out of it came a magnificent horse with three legs, strong and gleaming. It stood proudly on the shore, waiting.

Without hesitation, Malik and Kechal mounted the horse. It leaped into the water, galloping across the waves as if they were solid ground. In moments, they reached the other side.

They found another black stone, identical to the first. Kechal removed the reins and hid them beneath it. Nearby, they saw two pairs of iron shoes and two iron walking sticks.

They put on the iron shoes, picked up the staff, and began to walk.

The road ahead was unknown, but the bond between them had never been stronger.

The House Where Secrets Sleep

Wearing their iron shoes and leaning on the staff, Malik and Kechal Mamed walked for days. They journeyed in silence through forests that whispered secrets and meadows that shimmered like gold. The iron shoes grew thinner, and the staff wore down. Their legs ached, and their clothes grew ragged, but they pressed forward with quiet determination.

At last, when the soles of their shoes cracked, and the ends of their staffs splintered, they came upon a small wooden house at the edge of a sleepy village. Smoke curled from its crooked chimney. A fence of twisted branches surrounded it. A soft orange glow shone from its single window.

They approached the house, and before they could knock, the door creaked open. An old woman stood in the doorway. Her eyes were kind, and her back slightly bent with age. She wore a patched scarf and smiled as if she had been expecting them.

"Come in, travelers," she said. "You must be hungry and tired."

Malik bowed. "Grandma, we are weary and do not have much to offer. Could you let us rest here for the night?"

The woman stepped aside. " Certainly. There is always space here for kind hearts, but I must tell you, I have no food to offer."

"No worries," said Kechal, reaching into his bag. He pulled out a velvet pouch and handed her a ruby the size of a walnut. "Please take this. Use it to buy whatever you need."

The old woman's eyes widened, but she said nothing. She tucked the ruby into her large scarf and disappeared into the village. She returned a few hours later with a man carrying two large sacks, one full of food and the other brimming with coins.

The table was set, the fire rekindled, and soon, the house was filled with the warm smell of bread and stew. After the meal, Kechal leaned close to the woman and said, "Grandma, we need your help. We are looking for a place, the source of a secret we've traveled long to uncover."

She chuckled. "And what secret is that?"

"The secret of true friendship," Malik said.

The woman's eyes sparkled. "Ah. Then you've already been where you needed to go. The castle with invisible hands: the Fortress of the Three Elders. That was the place."

Malik blinked. "But they did not tell us the secret. They only sent us on this journey."

The woman nodded. "Yes. Because the journey itself is the answer. But if you still have doubts, there are two men in this village, Ahmed and Mamed, whose friendship has withstood every test. Visit them. See for yourselves."

Malik and Kechal thanked the kind woman and slept deeply for the first time in days. When the morning sun rose, they set out to find Ahmed and Mamed's house.

The Test of True Friends

It took nearly the whole morning to walk to the edge of the village, where a tall, stone house stood. Smoke drifted lazily from its chimney. Sheep grazed in a nearby pasture, and a shepherd greeted them warmly when they approached.

"Looking for the house of Ahmed and Mamed?" he said with a grin. "That's it, just there. I tend their flock. Good men, those two, were closer than brothers."

Malik and Kechal thanked him and knocked on the wooden door. A man with a strong build and warm eyes opened it. "Welcome," he said. "I'm Ahmed. Come in, be my guests. You are welcome here."

Inside, the house was clean and inviting, filled with the scent of warm bread and spices. Ahmed led them into a sitting room adorned with rugs and pillows.

"We've traveled far," Malik said, "seeking the secret of true friendship. They say you and Mamed know it."

Ahmed's face grew serious. "Before I share our story, you must tell me yours."

And so, Malik told it all; from the chest on the seashore to the golden fortress, the witch, the journey across the sea, and the iron shoes that had brought them to this very house.

Ahmed listened without interrupting. When Malik finished, Ahmed rose and called out, "Mamed! Come join us."

Mamed, thinner and older than Ahmed but with a gleam in his eye, entered the room and smiled. "More travelers?"

Ahmed waved him over. "These two want to hear our story."

The two old friends sat close to each other. Ahmed began.

"Years ago, I had dozens of friends, who laughed, feasted, and drank wine every night. My house was always full. One day, my father said to me: 'Son, you call them friends, but have you ever tested them?' I laughed it off. But father did not give up.

'My son,' he said, 'You are still very young. You cannot call everyone who smiles at you a friend. They're all your 'friends' while your pockets are full. Right now, we have wealth, and like flies to honey, they come swarming around. Most of them are here for the food, the drink. Do you really think they care about you? Try putting them to the test. Find out what's truly in their hearts.'

His words stuck with me. I decided to test them. One day, I slaughtered a lamb, stuffed it in a sack, and told my so-called friends I had accidentally killed the Shah's favorite ram. I asked for help hiding the body.

One by one, they refused. Some slammed doors in my face. Others told me never to return. I knocked on thirty-nine doors. All shut me out.

Discouraged, I passed by a small house belonging to Mamed. We were only distant acquaintances. But something told me to knock. He opened the door, listened, and then said, 'Let's go. Let's bury it on the outskirts of the town.' He dug the grave and even carried the sack when I could no longer stand. He helped me redirect a nearby stream over the grave to hide all traces of it. I knew then that I had found my true friend.

Mamed chuckled. "And then he tested me again!"

Ahmed nodded. "Later, I lost everything. I went searching for Mamed. He was now a wealthy merchant in another city. When I asked him for help, he barely looked at me, tossed a few coins my way, and walked off. I was hurt.

But that night, a kind woman and her daughter found my sister and me and took us in. They fed us and gave us a room. Later, a man came claiming to owe my father money and gave us two bags of gold. Life started to turn around.

Eventually, I ran into Mamed at the marketplace. I tried to walk past him as if I did not notice him, but he called out to me,

'Ahmed, are you upset with me?'

What could I say? I said,

'Of course I am upset. You did not behave like a true friend. When I came to you in need and asked for help, you did not even look at me, didn't ask how I was doing. Is that how a friend behaves?'

Mamed frowned and responded,

'Everything you said is true, Ahmed. I gave you money without even looking at you. I won't deny it. But I did not turn my back on our friendship. I treated you like a stranger because you looked like a beggar, and my wife never would've believed that someone in rags could be my friend. But after that, I sent my mother to find you. She brought you into our home and treated you like her own son. A little later, I sent my father, and he gave you two purses of gold. '

My guests, you should know, every word he said was accurate. And from that moment on, I understood my friend. Our bond only grew stronger, and from that day forward, we were never apart again."

Malik and Kechal listened in silence, deeply moved by the story.

"This," Ahmed said, "is the secret of true friendship. It is not just loyalty, but sacrifice, patience, and trust even when things aren't what they seem."

The sun had long set. Malik and Kechal thanked the men and spent the night in their home, feeling they had finally learned what they had come for.

Return Through the Seven Kingdoms

With their hearts full and their questions answered, Malik and Kechal Mamed set out at dawn. The road home would take them through seven kingdoms, each with its Shah, its customs, and its dangers.

Their first days were easy. They crossed blooming meadows and gentle hills, with farmers offering them water and bread along the way. But soon, word spread across the region that two travelers carried stories and riches from faraway lands. Some viewed them as heroes, while others considered them targets.

In the fourth kingdom, they came upon a narrow mountain pass. As they entered the rocky trail, bandits leaped from behind the boulders. It was an ambush. The leader pointed a curved sword at them and said, "Hand over everything."

Malik stood tall. "We have nothing but knowledge. But if you value wisdom over gold, listen to what we've learned."

Curious, the bandits lowered their weapons. Malik and Kechal told them of the Fortress of the Three Elders, the journey across the sea, and what it truly meant to be a friend.

When they finished, the leader, a grizzled man with a scar across his cheek, nodded slowly. "I've had a friend like that once. Lost him in battle." He signaled the others. "Let them go. They do not have gold coins, but their story is priceless."

Word of their story traveled faster than they did. By the time they reached the sixth kingdom, people were waiting along the roads, hoping to hear the tale of the prince and the clever wanderer.

In every village, someone would ask, "Is it true? You faced a witch? Crossed the sea on a three-legged horse? Walked in iron shoes?"

And Malik would smile. "Yes, but the greatest trial was learning what true friendship means."

At last, they reached the border of their homeland. The towers of the royal palace shimmered in the distance.

News of their return had already reached the capital. The Shah himself came out to greet them, surrounded by the royal court and a hundred cheering townspeople. Trumpets blared, and drums rolled.

The Shah stepped forward and embraced his son. "You are not just my son and heir anymore. You've become a man whose heart is wiser than any king's crown." Then he turned to Kechal Mamed and said, "And you, my brave companion. You stood by his side through every trial. Ask for anything, and it shall be yours."

Kechal bowed his head in a gesture of respect and humility. "All I ask is that our story be remembered, and that no one ever forgets what true friendship means."

The Shah nodded. "Then let the tale of Malik and Kechal be told for generations."

And so, for seven days and nights, the kingdom celebrated. Feasts were held in every village. The storyteller sang of the journey. Malik and Kechal remained close as brothers. One wore a crown, the other a plain robe, but their bond was equal. For in the heart of every true friend, no rank or riches matter. Somewhere, in the golden Fortress of the Three Elders, three wise men smiled.

True friendship isn't proven when times are easy, but during the journey through trials, doubts, and hardship. Real friends walk beside you when the path is most challenging.

Seven Sticks

ong ago, there lived an old man who had seven sons. They did everything together: ate, worked, laughed, played, and even went hunting side by side. They were so close that nothing, not even wild beasts, could break their bond.

But time passed. The boys grew up, got married, and had children of their own. Each started building his own home, tending to his own life, and, little by little, they stopped visiting one another.

Their strong bond began to fade.

The old man, now grey and weak, lived alone. His sons still came to see him sometimes, but something was missing. They no longer laughed together and helped each other.

The joy of brotherhood was gone.

One day, the father called all his sons to his side.

"My children," he said, "tomorrow, I want each of you to bring me a pomegranate stick as thick as your finger."

The next day, the sons returned, each holding a smooth, sturdy stick. The old man took the seven sticks and tied them tightly into one thick bundle.

"Now," he said, "let's see if any of you can break this bundle."

Each son tried, one by one, twisting, bending, pulling, but no one could break the sticks tied together.

Then, the father untied the bundle and handed each son a single stick.

"Try now," he said.

Snap! Each stick broke easily, one after the other.

The sons looked at their father, puzzled.

"These seven sticks," the father said, "are like you, seven brothers. When you stay together, no one can break you. But when you go your separate ways, like these single sticks, you are easy to snap."

From that day forward, the brothers remembered their father's words. They helped one another, visited often, and lived once again in peace and harmony.

The old man spent the rest of his days with a peaceful heart, watching his sons care for one another as they had once done. Their homes were filled with laughter, their children played together like brothers and sisters, and no problem was ever too big when they faced it as one family.

Whenever someone in the village felt lonely or quarreled with a sibling, they were reminded of the story of unity and strength involving seven sticks.

Together, we are unbreakable, but divided, we fall.

The Tale of Saleh and Valeh

Long ago, in the city of Ganja, there lived two poor brothers named Saleh and Valeh. One day, feeling tired of living in poverty, Saleh said to his younger brother:

"Let's leave this place and try our fortune elsewhere."

Valeh agreed, and the two set off across mountains and valleys until they arrived in a distant city. There, they found work with two different shopkeepers.

Valeh, ever humble and hardworking, made a deal to serve his employer for one year. At the end of the year, he counted his earnings with the shopkeeper: twelve copper coins.

"Would you like to stay another year?" the shopkeeper asked.

Valeh agreed and stayed. A second year passed, and again, they earned twelve coins. Still, Valeh remained loyal. After a third year, the same sum was counted again.

Just then, Saleh came to find Valeh.

"Brother," he said, "I'm heading home. Come with me."

"With what money?" Valeh asked. "I only have eighteen copper coins."

"I have five hundred gold pieces," said Saleh proudly. "I will return home wealthy man. At least you could buy something for your children, and I will take it to them."

Valeh agreed. At the market, he purchased a bag of sweet raisins, roasted chickpeas, and sugared almonds. Just as he was leaving, he noticed a poor boy in rags eyeing his small gifts.

Feeling pity for the boy, Valeh gave him some from each bag. In return, the boy silently placed a small stone in Valeh's hand and vanished. It was now a ruby, a rare red gemstone!

Valeh ran, trying to find the boy, but he was gone. He found Saleh.

"Give this ruby to my wife," he said. "Tell her to sell it and feed the children. I will return once my work-contract ends."

Saleh took the gem and returned to Ganja. Valeh's wife, desperate and poor, ran to him.

"Where is my husband?"

"Unfortunately, he passed away in a road incident," Saleh blatantly lied to Valeh's wife.

"Oh no, what? How will I feed the children?"

"That is not my concern," he replied coldly.

Time passed. One day, Valeh's master asked him to bring some water. As Valeh drew from a well, he accidentally loosened a brick. Beneath it, he found a box filled with priceless rubies, the same, red-colored gemstones!

Fearful of being seen as a thief, Valeh immediately informed his master.

"I found this but did not touch it."

The master smiled and said, "Your honesty is worth more than these gemstones. Please take some rubies and travel home to see your family."

Valeh sold one ruby, bought gifts, and returned to his hometown. He decided to stay in a *caravanserai* for a few days to learn what had happened to his family.

One day, the Shah overheard a well-dressed man named Valeh speaking to a beggar woman. She was his wife, worn and poor.

"Are you Valeh's wife?" he asked gently.

"Yes," she said. "But he died on the road. That is what his surviving brother told."

"Did you at least receive a ruby from him?"

"No," she replied.

"I think you should go to the Shah," Valeh advised, "and tell him everything that happened. You can count me as your witness."

The woman followed his advice. The Shah summoned Saleh.

"Why did you lie and steal from your brother's family?"

Saleh protested. "I gave her the ruby. I have witnesses!"

Then, he brought several false witnesses.

At that moment, the bald Shah summoned the judge and said:

"Let me judge this myself. Bring everyone involved to me."

He created clay models of a watermelon, a melon, a gourd, and a cucumber and laid them in front of the witnesses. Each witness was asked, "How does the shape of the ruby compare to the clay models you see in front of you?"

One said, "Like a gourd."

Another, "As big as a melon."

Another, "Long like a cucumber."

They all disagreed and gave the wrong colors: blue, white, and yellow.

Then Valeh's turn came, and he was asked.

"It was small, like a prayer bead. But it changed colors and glowed in the dark."

The Shah turned to the judge.

"The truth is clear. Now we will do what is just and fair."

The Shah ordered Saleh and his false witnesses to be punished and return the stolen wealth to Valeh's wife.

That evening, Valeh quietly entered his old home. His wife, not recognizing him, offered him a plate of pilaf.

"Thank you," he said. "But I am your husband, Valeh."

She looked closely and wept with joy when she realized it was Valeh, alive and well.

They lived in peace, their hardships behind them.

Truth may take a winding road, but it always finds its way, because even the greatest lie has an expiration date.

The Story of Fatima

The Golden Cow

ong time ago, in a quiet village surrounded by hills and orchards, a kind man lived with his sweet little daughter, Fatima. She had bright, olive-colored eyes and a smile as warm as the sun.

Fatima's mother had passed when she was just a child, but the girl grew up kind and full of joy. She helped her father with every task, never once complaining. Their home was small but warm. There was a fig tree in the yard, carpets on the floor, and a golden cow that glowed like the setting sun and was as gentle as a lullaby song.

The cow wasn't special just for her golden coat; she helped Fatima in quiet, magical ways that no one else knew. When Fatima sat to spin wool, the golden cow would gently chew the tangled fibers, soften them with her warm breath, and spit them out perfectly clean and fluffy.

Fatima whispered, "Thank you," and patted her friend's head.

But those peaceful days did not last forever.

One morning, Fatima's father took her hand and said gently,

"Every child needs a mother's care. I've found someone, and we'll be getting married."

Soon after, a woman arrived with her daughter.

Fatima smiled and welcomed them kindly, hoping for a warm new family. But the stepmother was cold, and her daughter was rough and lazy. She never helped with a anything. She laughed too loudly, ate more than her share, and watched while Fatima worked from dawn to dusk.

Yet Fatima did not complain. She swept the floors, fetched water, gathered firewood, and spun wool with tired fingers.

She found comfort in the golden cow, quiet and gentle, helping her behind the scenes.

It did not take long for the stepmother to grow suspicious. She did not like how Fatima always managed to finish her chores so neatly. She watched the golden cow closely and grew jealous.

One day, she lay down on the floor with a groan and pretended to be sick. "Oh, I feel awful," she moaned, pressing a hand to her head.

Fatima's father rushed to her side. "What's wrong, my dear? What can I do to make you feel better?"

"Only one thing will save me," she whispered. "I must wrap myself in the hide of a golden cow, the only way to get rid of my fever."

The father frowned. He did not want to hurt the cow, but he did not want his wife to suffer and was afraid of losing her, too.

When Fatima heard the plan, her heart sank. She ran to the barn, wrapped her arms around the cow's neck, and cried.

But the golden cow looked at her kindly and said,

"Do not cry, dear Fatima. That is my fate. Now, listen closely. Do not eat my meat. Gather my bones, take them to the barn, and bury them carefully. Someday, you will need me, and I will come."

Fatima kissed her on the forehead and made a promise.

The next day, the cow was gone. Fatima kept her promise, buried the bones in the barnyard earth with tears in her eyes.

And from that day forward, life only grew harder.

A Sad Goodbye

After the golden cow was gone, Fatima's days became longer and lonelier.

The stepmother wasted no time. She loaded Fatima's hands with more wool than ever before; dirty, tangled, and rough. "Finish this by nightfall," she barked. "No excuses!"

Fatima tried, but without the golden cow's help, the wool twisted and knotted. Her fingers ached, her back hurt, and her eyes filled with tears. And whenever Fatima couldn't keep up, the stepmother would yell, or worse, wave a stick and shout, "Lazy girl! you will never be good for anything!"

Fatima never responded. She held her tongue and worked twice as hard.

One morning, she took the wool to the meadow where the golden cow once grazed. She sat on a low hill, spinning and sighing.

Suddenly, a sharp breeze swept through the field. It lifted the wool from her lap and sent it flying.

"Wait!" Fatima cried. "Come back!"

The wool tumbled through the air like a white butterfly, and Fatima ran after it.

"Kind wind, please do not take it," she pleaded. "I will get in so much trouble!"

But the wind did not listen. It carried the wool even farther. Fatima chased it until the village disappeared behind her.

Fatima ran past trees, over stones, through tall grass, and soon found herself in a wide valley she had never seen before.

At the edge of the valley, a quiet river flowed. And beside it stood a crooked little house made of gray stone and crooked wood. Smoke curled from its chimney, and strange herbs hung from its windows.

Fatima's wool danced one last time in the air, and disappeared straight down the chimney.

She took a breath, stepped to the door, and knocked.

What or who waited inside, she did not know.

The Strange Old Woman

The door creaked open.

Inside the little house, shadows danced on the walls. In the corner, near a low-burning fire, sat the strangest old woman Fatima had ever seen.

Her face was long and wrinkled, with eyes round as plums and a mouth so wide it nearly reached her ears. Her teeth looked like crooked nails, and her hair stuck out like dried grass.

Fatima froze. Her heart still thudded like a drum as she ran for a while after her wool.

The old woman looked up and smiled.

"Come in, child," she said gently. "Do not be afraid. You must be tired. You've run a long way."

Fatima hesitated. The woman's smile did not seem scary. In fact, it reminded her of her grandmother's.

"I think your wool flew into my chimney," the woman said, pointing towards it. "Stay with me a day or two. Help around the house, and I will give it back."

Fatima slowly stepped inside.

"Sit with me a while," the old woman said. "What's your name?"

"Fatima."

"Fatima," the old woman repeated with a nod. "Will you help me with something, dear? My old head itches terribly. Will you look through my hair?"

Fatima sat down beside her. The woman laid her head on the girl's lap. Her hair was tangled and full of dust, but Fatima did not complain. She had seen worse; her stepmother never brushed her hair either.

As she worked, the old woman asked, "Tell me, whose head is cleaner: mine or your mother's?"

Fatima paused. Then kindly answered, "Yours, Granny. Yours is much cleaner."

The old woman smiled again.

"You must be hungry," she said. "There's bread in that barrel. Take a piece for yourself."

Fatima opened the barrel but inside was only a lump of clay.

Still, she smiled and said, "It's so soft, Granny. Thank you. But let me make you a fresh loaf. You should rest. I will take care of the house."

The old woman leaned back and watched. Fatima swept the floor, tidied the shelves, and baked warm, soft bread in the oven. They ate together, and for the first time in days, Fatima felt full and peaceful.

That night, she told the old woman everything about her stepmother, the golden cow, and how hard she worked.

The woman listened quietly, and in the morning, she said, "It's time for you to go home, child. But listen carefully..."

The Three Rivers

Before Fatima stepped outside, the old woman handed the ball of wool back to her.

"You kept your heart kind and your words gentle," she said. "Now, remember this: on your way home, you will come across three rivers. Each one is special."

She leaned closer and whispered:

"Bathe in the white river, and it will wash away all your worries.

Bend to the black river, and it will make your hair shine like night.

Dip your cheeks in the red river, and your face will glow like a rose in bloom."

Fatima thanked her with a grateful heart and began her journey back.

Soon, she came upon the first river, the white, clear and cool. She stepped in, and a calm washed over her like a quiet breeze.

Next came the black river, dark and smooth as silk. Fatima knelt and rinsed her hair. It gleamed in the sunlight.

Last was the red river, glowing like a sunset. She cupped the water in her hands and touched it to her cheeks.

When Fatima rose from the riverside, something had changed. Her reflection in the water shimmered: her eyes were brighter, her skin glowed, and her hair shone like a midnight sky.

She looked like a girl from a famous painting, but still, the same kind, hardworking Fatima was inside.

And with the wool in her hands and hope in her step, she made her way back home.

The Jealous Stepmother

When Fatima returned home, her stepmother was waiting by the door, arms crossed and eyes sharp.

But the moment she saw Fatma, she gasped.

The girl's face glowed like a flower at dawn. Her hair shone like satin. Even her simple clothes seemed touched by magic.

The stepmother's heart twisted with jealousy.

"What took you so long?" she snapped, trying to hide her surprise. But she couldn't stop staring. Her daughter, lazy and rough, had never looked anything like this.

She pulled Fatima aside.

"What happened to you?" she demanded. "Where did you go? What did you do?"

Fatima, kind as always, told the truth. She told her about the runaway wool, the strange little house, the old woman, and the three rivers.

The stepmother listened carefully to every word, twisting it into a greedy thought in her mind.

That night, she turned to her daughter and said, "Tomorrow, you will follow her path. you will go to that same house. Do what she did and come back more beautiful than ever."

The girl, grumpy and sleepy, groaned. "Do I have to?"

"If you want to look like Fatima, yes!" her mother hissed.

And so, without understanding what kindness truly meant, the stepmother sent her daughter off into the world, expecting the same magic to return.

The Lazy Girl's Journey

The next morning, the stepmother shoved a bundle of wool into her daughter's hands and pointed down the road.

"Go straight to the house," she warned. "Do not dawdle. Do not wander. And do not come back without a new face!"

Muttering under her breath, the girl stumped away.

She did not walk far before a sudden gust of wind snatched the wool from her hands. It flew into the sky like a kite and drifted out of sight.

"Ugh, great," she muttered and chased after it, not because she cared, but because she did not want to get scolded again.

Just like with Fatima, the wool led her to the strange little house by the river. Smoke curled from the chimney. The crooked wooden door stood slightly open.

She stepped inside and froze.

In the corner sat a wrinkled old woman with wild gray hair and a mouth so wide it nearly touched both ears. Her eyes were round and bulging, and her arms were long enough to stretch across the room.

The girl turned to run away, but her mother's voice echoed in her head: "Do not come back without a new face!"

So, she took a deep breath and stepped inside.

The old woman smiled. "Welcome, child. Looking for your wool? Stay a day or two, help me around the house, and you will have it back."

The girl rolled her eyes. "Fine."

She slumped into a chair and crossed her arms.

"Would you comb my hair, child?" the old woman asked gently. "It hasn't been touched in ages."

The girl sighed. "Gross."

Still, she sat down and put the old woman's head on her lap, but the moment she saw the tangled mess, she wrinkled her nose and shoved it away.

"Yuck. it is like a bird's nest!"

The old woman's eyes narrowed slightly, but she said nothing.

Later, she told the girl, "If you are hungry, take some bread from the barrel."

The girl lifted the lid and saw only a lump of clay.

"This is your bread?" she sneered. "My mom bakes better stuff in her sleep."

Still, the old woman stayed calm. "If you do not like it, you can make a fresh loaf."

"What else?!" the girl barked. "You do it."

Instead of helping or working, she sprawled out on the bench, complaining and bossing, while the old woman watched in silence.

That night, the girl did nothing. The next morning, she stood up and said, "Well? Where's my beauty?"

The old woman smiled thinly. "You may go, child. On your way, you will see three rivers: one black, one red, and one white. Wash your face in the black one, your arms in the red one, and your hair in the white."

Without saying thank you, the girl snatched her wool and stomped off.

She did not listen closely. She dipped in the wrong rivers, washed her hair in the black, her face in the red, and ignored the white one completely.

By the time she got home, her hair was sticky, her skin had darkened with strange patches, and her frown had somehow deepened.

Her mother ran to greet her, then gasped in horror.

"Is that… you?!"

The girl burst into tears, but it was too late. Kindness, it seemed, did not work its magic on the lazy or the proud.

The Wedding Invitation

Life became even harder for Fatima after her stepsister returned. Now that her beauty shone brighter than ever, the stepmother's jealousy burned like fire. She barked orders, gave cruel punishments, and kept Fatima hidden away from the world.

But one day, the village buzzed with excitement. A wedding was being held in a nearby town, and everyone was invited.

The stepmother dressed her daughter in her finest clothes, silks that did not fit right and colors that clashed, and then began preparing herself. She brushed her hair, fixed her scarf, and added too much perfume.

Fatima watched from the corner and whispered, "Please, may I come too? I promise I will be quiet and help with all the chores when we get back."

"Ha!" the stepmother scoffed. "You? At a wedding? You will embarrass us all. Stay here and make yourself useful!"

Then she dumped a heavy jar of buckwheat on the floor and barked, "Sort these grains one by one. Every single one! Or else."

With that, she took her daughter's hand and marched out the door, leaving Fatima alone.

Tears welled in Fatima's eyes as she stared at the huge mess. She knelt beside it and began picking grains, one seed at a time. But no matter how fast she worked, the pile never seemed to shrink.

Just then, she heard a familiar cluck.

It was the speckled rooster that she always fed and cared for in the yard. The rooster shuffled over, cocked his head, and asked with soft human voice, "Why are you crying, dear Fatima?"

Fatima explained between sniffles.

The rooster fluffed her feathers proudly. "Do not worry. We'll help!"

He gave a loud cluck-a-doodle! Suddenly, all the hens, roosters, and even the tiny chicks came rushing in. In no time, they were pecking through the grains, sorting them faster than any hands could.

Fatima laughed through her tears.

Then she tiptoed to the barn and dug up the hidden bundle of bones from her golden cow, the ones she had buried just as the cow had asked.

She held them in her hands and whispered the special words.

A soft glow surrounded her.

In a flash, a beautiful golden gown appeared, along with a pair of sparkling slippers. She twirled once, and her reflection shimmered like the morning sun on the water.

A voice whispered gently, "Go, sweet Fatima. But return before your stepmother comes home."

And just like that, Fatima hurried off to the wedding.

When she entered the gathering, all eyes turned to her. No one recognized the radiant girl with glowing cheeks, graceful steps, and a dress that shimmered like stardust.

People whispered, "Who is she?"

The bride begged her to stay. The musicians played faster. And when Fatima danced, she floated across the floor like a breeze across a field.

From the far corner of the hall, the prince watched in awe as the mysterious girl, who moved like moonlight, came to life. Curiosity tugged at his heart, and he slipped through the crowd. But just as he drew near, Fatima darted away, quick as a deer.

Before the sun could set, she slipped away, rushing home so fast that she did not notice that one of her golden slippers had fallen behind.

She returned just in time, changed out of her dress, and resumed her chores with a quiet smile.

The stepmother came home, huffing and puffing, dragging her daughter, who had spilled soup on her dress and danced like a sleepy goose.

"Did you finish?" the stepmother barked.

Fatima nodded.

The buckwheat was sorted perfectly. The house was neat. And the stepmother grew suspicious.

But she said nothing yet.

Because something was about to happen, something that would change Fatma's life forever.

The Lost Slipper

The next morning, whispers spread like wind through the village:

At the wedding, someone had found a slipper. It was not just any slipper, but one unlike anything anyone had ever seen.

It was embroidered with golden thread, light as air, and so perfectly made that the prince himself could not stop staring at it.

"Whose slipper is this?" he asked his men.

No one knew her name or where she had gone, but everyone insisted the slipper belonged to the enchanting stranger who danced like starlight and vanished in a heartbeat. Hope ignited in the prince's heart, and, at last, he held a clue to find the mysterious girl who had stolen his breath. So, the prince made a royal decree:

"Search every town, every home. When you find the girl this slipper fits, bring her to the palace. I must meet her."

The prince's messengers went from village to village, knocking on doors and asking to try the slipper on every girl.

But it was never the correct size.

Some girls had feet that were too long. Others are too wide. Some squeezed and twisted, trying to force it on, but the slipper refused to fit.

Finally, the messengers reached the village where Fatima lived.

The stepmother saw them coming from the window. She rushed to her daughter, washed her face, and stuffed her into her best clothes.

"Sit up straight!" she hissed. "Smile sweetly. It is your chance!"

Then she turned to Fatima, tied her hands with string, stuffed a stone in her mouth, and shoved her into the *tandır* hiding her away.

When the messengers arrived, they tried the slipper on the stepsister. But her foot was too large, and her face too sour.

The slipper simply would not fit.

Just as the men turned to leave, a loud crowing broke the silence.

"Cock-a-doodle-doo! Look in the tandır. She's hidden from you!"

Startled, the messengers looked around. The speckled rooster was flapping on the fence, crowing louder and louder:

"Cock-a-doodle-doo! Fatima's in the tandır tied up, too!"

The men rushed to the clay oven. They opened the heavy lid, and gasped.

There, sat Fatima, dusty but beautiful, her hands tied, a stone in her mouth, her eyes wide with surprise.

They freed her gently.

Then, one of them knelt and offered her the golden slipper. It slid on her foot as if it had always belonged there.

"I think this is yours," he said.

Fatima nodded, then ran to the stable and returned with the matching slipper in her hands.

The messengers smiled. "We've found her."

And they brought Fatima to the palace just as the prince had asked.

The Prince's Choice

When Fatima arrived at the palace, the halls were already buzzing with excitement.

The prince waited in the grand courtyard, and as soon as he saw her, his face lit up. She was the girl from the wedding, the one who had danced like a starlight and vanished like a dream.

Fatima bowed politely, unsure of what to do. But the prince stepped forward and said,

"You lost something precious the night we met. I am so glad we've found you."

Fatima blushed but stood tall. "Thank you, Your Highness."

The prince looked at his advisors. "There's no need for a ball or contest. She is the one I've been searching for."

The palace was filled with cheers. Preparations for the wedding began at once.

As for Fatima, she asked for just one thing before the ceremony:

"To visit my old home, one last time."

With the prince's permission, she returned, but this time, not in rags or sorrow, but in royal splendor.

The villagers stared as she rode by, dressed in silk and gold, kindness shining in her eyes.

The stepmother and her daughter peeked from their window and fainted in shock.

Fatima could have spoken harshly. She could have asked for revenge.

But instead, she simply said,

"I forgive you. May you both find peace."

And with that, she turned away, never looking back.

That very week, the prince and Fatima were married in a joyful celebration. Guests came from every corner of the kingdom. The feast lasted for seven days and nights, with music, laughter, and dancing in the gardens.

Fatima never forgot the golden cow, the hens who helped her, the kind old woman in the valley, or the courage it took to keep going. She ruled beside the prince with wisdom and grace, and her story was told for generations.

Kindness, patience, and honesty may not bring immediate rewards, but in the end, they always shine the brightest.

The Rusty Sword

A Shah's Last Words

Long ago, in the city of Isfahan, a wise and aging Shah resided. He had ruled well and raised three sons: Ahmad, the eldest; Mahmud, the middle son; and Hasan, the youngest.

One day, feeling the weight of old age and knowing his time was near, the Shah called his sons to his bedside.

"My children," he said, "I do not have much time left. Listen carefully to what I am about to say."

He turned to each of them in turn.

"Ahmad, I leave the throne to you. Mahmud will serve as your Vizir. And Hasan, though you are the youngest, I appoint you as my royal advisor because you possess both courage and intelligence."

He paused, then added something they did not expect.

"There is one more thing. In the 40th room of the palace, behind seven locked doors, there is a chest. Inside it lies an old, rusty sword. If you ever set out on a long and dangerous journey, take that sword with you. With it by your side, no enemy will be able to defeat you."

Having spoken his last wish, the Shah closed his eyes and passed away.

The Journey of Prince Ahmad

After the king's death, Ahmad became ruler. At first, he governed wisely. However, over time, palace life grew boring, and he decided to explore distant lands. He handed his duties to Mahmud, gathered his army, and prepared to leave.

Just as he was about to set off, Hasan stepped forward.

"Brother, remember Father's last wish," he reminded him. "You are going on a long journey. Take the rusty sword."

Ahmad laughed.

"You are serious?" he said. "Father was old and rambled nonsense. What would people say if their Shah traveled with a rusty old blade? They would laugh at their king. I am giving that sword to you."

And with that, he rode away without it.

He traveled far and wide until he came upon a strange and beautiful fortress surrounded by a thick forest of towering trees. Ahmad had never seen a place so grand.

He ordered his men to rest, and the next morning he approached the fortress. The gates were locked, but Ahmad was not going to allow closed doors to stop him. He broke through them and stepped inside.

What he saw took his breath away: lush gardens filled with flowers, nightingales singing on every bush, and in the center, a grand pool built from bricks of gold and silver. Seventy-seven fountains poured crystal-clear water into it, but not a soul was in sight.

Ahmad, feeling bold, undressed to bathe. But the moment his foot touched the water, the sky darkened, thunder roared, lightning flashed, and from the storm a warrior descended on a horse with wings.

"How dare you enter my garden?" the warrior thundered. "You will be punished. I will strike you where you stand!"

Before Ahmad could react, the warrior drew his sword and, in a single flash, ended the prince's life. Then he vanished into the sky as quickly as he had come.

Mahmud's Fate

Weeks passed, and there was still no word from Prince Ahmad. His brother Mahmud grew worried. At last, he gathered a small army and set out to find him.

Just like Ahmad, Mahmud ignored their father's last request. He, too, left the rusty sword behind.

After a long and weary journey, Mahmud reached the same mysterious fortress. As he approached, his heart sank. There, lying beneath the outer wall, was Ahmad's lifeless body.

The fortress was strange and unsettling. Its walls, now seen up close, appeared to be built from the skulls of fallen men. Mahmud turned pale and considered retreating.

But before he could move, thunder rolled across the sky. Dark clouds swept in, and a deafening roar echoed through the forest. From above, the same winged horse descended, bearing the same masked warrior.

"How dare you enter my garden?" the warrior shouted, drawing a gleaming sword.

Mahmud tried to defend himself, but he was no match for him. The warrior struck, and in a flash, Mahmud met the same fate as his older brother. His body was laid beside Ahmad's, and the fortress returned to silence.

Hasan's Quest

At home in Isfahan, the youngest brother, Prince Hasan, waited anxiously. Weeks turned into months, and there was no sign of either Ahmad or Mahmud.

Unlike his brothers, Hasan was not only strong but also wise. He remembered his father's final words and took them to heart.

Before setting off, he visited his mother to ask for her blessing. She hugged him tightly and said:

"Hasan, my son, your path will not be easy. But take this with you—it is your father's gift."

She unlocked the chest in the 40th room and carefully unwrapped the old, rusty sword. Its blade was dull, but the moment Hasan fastened it to his belt, he felt a surge of strength in his arms.

"One more thing," his mother said. "If you meet someone in need along the way, do not look the other way. Help them with all your heart. Only then will good fortune stay with you."

Hasan took a small army and set out on his journey. Days passed. Then weeks. And finally, he reached the same eerie fortress.

The moment he saw the walls, towering and built from human bones, he knew his brothers had met their end here.

Inside the gates, he found their cloaks and armor scattered near the golden pool. Grief welled up in his chest. But before he could begin searching for their bodies, a storm erupted overhead. Thunder cracked. A black cloud rolled in, and from it descended the winged horse and its rider, just as before.

But Hasan did not flinch. As the warrior landed, he shouted the familiar words, "How dare you enter my garden?" Hasan gripped his father's sword and stood tall.

"Do not say a word, coward," Hasan replied. "You killed my brothers, and now I've come to end your evil. Let's finish this!"

The warrior unsheathed their sword, and the two clashed.

Their battle raged for forty days and forty nights, shaking the earth and splitting the sky. No side could gain the upper hand, until, on the forty-first day, Hasan struck a final blow and sent the warrior crashing to the ground.

The warrior's helmet rolled away, and to Hasan's astonishment, it revealed not a man, but a young woman of stunning beauty.

In that moment, his strength vanished, and the world around him faded. Hasan fainted.

When he woke, the garden was empty. But beside him lay a scrap of parchment, with delicate writing in a language he could read:

"I am Peri, daughter of the Frankish King. My father tried to force me into marriage, but I swore I would wed only the one who could defeat me in battle. That man is you.

If you wish, come seek me. Ask for my hand. I will be waiting."

Hasan pressed the note to his heart. He knew what he had to do.

He returned home, told his mother everything, and placed the kingdom in the care of the Vizir. Then, with the rusty sword still strapped to his side, he mounted his horse and set out, this time, not for revenge or duty, but for love.

The Giant and the Splinter

Hasan rode for days through mountains and forests, asking for directions to the land of the Franks, but no one had ever heard of such a place. Still, he pressed on.

Then one day, he reached a clearing in the woods and froze.

There, lying in the grass, was a massive Deev, a giant so large that the earth seemed to tremble with every breath he took. The Deev groaned in pain, clutching his leg, and each moan sent flocks of birds flying from the trees.

Hasan approached carefully and saw the problem: a huge wooden splinter, like an entire tree branch, was stuck deep in the giant's foot. The wound was swollen, and blood pulsed with every heartbeat.

Hasan wanted to help, but he was cautious.

"What if the Deev wakes up and crushes me?" he thought. "I need a plan."

So, he dug a shallow pit beneath the Deev's leg, covered it with brush, and climbed in. From this hidden spot, he began pulling at the splinter.

The Deev jolted in pain and roared:

"Who's torturing me? Show yourself! If I catch you, I will tear you to pieces!"

But Hasan did not stop. He gave one last tug, and the splinter slid free. Blood poured from the wound, and the Deev slumped with a sigh of relief… and fell into a deep, peaceful sleep.

Hours later, the Deev woke up. He flexed his leg and stood tall, completely healed. Surprised, he looked around.

"Who helped me?" he shouted. "Come out, whoever you are! I promise, I will repay you with all my heart."

Hasan climbed out of the pit.

The Deev's eyes widened. He bent to one knee and said,

"O son of man, you saved me from death. Tell me, what can I do for you?"

Hasan replied,

"I do not want gold or treasures. I want a brother. Be my friend and help me find the land of the Franks. I seek a woman named Peri, the daughter of their king."

The Deev was beaming.

"Brother! Nothing would make me prouder. I do not know where the Frankish kingdom lies, but I know someone who might."

With that, he bent low and said,

"Climb on. We'll fly."

The Brothers of the Sky

With Hasan riding on his back, the great Deev leapt into the sky. They soared over rivers and valleys, cities and deserts, until they came to a vast forest. There, nestled among ancient trees, stood a grand palace carved from white stone.

Sitting at the gates was a giant white Deev, even larger than the one who had carried Hasan. When he saw them approach, the white Deev grinned hungrily.

"Ah, brother!" he bellowed. "Welcome back. It has been ages, and I see you've brought dinner! I was just starting to crave a bit of roasted human."

Hasan tensed, but his Deev-friend stepped in front of him.

"This man is not a meal," he said firmly. "He saved my life. He is my brother now. If you touch him, I will take our case to Father, and I will never speak to you again."

The white Deev blinked in surprise, then broke into a booming laugh.

"Well, why did not you say so? If he is your brother, then he is my brother too!"

He scooped Hasan up gently, lifted him to eye level, and kissed both his cheeks as a customary greeting.

They feasted that night, and Hasan told them his story: how he had won a battle against a warrior who turned out to be Princess Peri, and how he now searched for her homeland, the kingdom of the Franks.

But the white Deev only shook his head.

"I have never heard of this place," he admitted. "But our eldest brother, the gray Deev, might know. he is the wisest among us. You should go to him."

The next morning, Hasan and his Deev-friend flew off again. This time, they crossed snowy mountains, thundering waterfalls, and golden fields. Finally, they spotted a rocky hill with a silver palace at its base. Guarding the palace sat the gray Deev, older and larger than the others, his beard trailing like smoke and his eyes like twin moons.

When he saw them land, he chuckled.

"So, my little brothers return! Have you brought me a treat?"

"No," said the younger Deev. "We've brought our brother."

Hasan stepped forward, bowed, and told his story once more.

The gray Deev listened closely, then slowly nodded.

"Yes… I have heard of the land you seek. The Frankish kingdom lies far beyond these lands, across wild plains and hidden rivers."

Then he took a small piece of wool from his robe and handed it to Hasan.

"If you are ever in danger, burn this wool, and I will come to your aid," he said.

Hasan nodded and, in return, took out a dagger and gave it to the Deev.

"If the blade begins to bleed, know that I am in trouble. Come find me."

The Deev smiled and tucked the dagger into his belt.

Then, with a final embrace, Hasan said farewell to his Deev brothers and set off alone, now on foot, but closer than ever to finding Peri.

The Goose Keeper and the Garden of Dreams

After many days of travel, Hasan came upon a quiet pasture where a lone shepherd tended his flock. Tired, dusty, and unsure how close he was to the Frankish kingdom, Hasan greeted him kindly.

"Peace be upon you, shepherd. Can you sell me a sheep for the road?"

The shepherd looked closely at Hasan and smiled. "You must be a traveler from far away. In our land, we do not sell to strangers, we honor them. Take any sheep you like, it is my gift."

Hasan bowed in gratitude and selected a young ram. After using what he could from the animal to feed himself, he fashioned a clever disguise by drying and shaping the inner structure of the animal into a makeshift hood. After he pulled the garment over his head and shoulders, he looked just like a bald beggar, which was exactly what he needed to move unnoticed.

Soon, he reached the capital city of the Frankish kingdom. In the center of the town stood a magnificent garden, filled with fruit trees, rare birds, and shimmering fountains. Hasan snuck inside, bathed in one of the pools, ate some figs, and fell asleep under a tree.

By dawn, the king's guards had found him.

They hauled him before the throne. The Frankish Shah wearing a heavy golden crown, glared down.

"Who are you, beggar? How dare you trespass in the royal garden?"

Hasan bowed low. "Your Majesty, I am no thief. I am a traveler with no home. I was tired, and the garden seemed so peaceful."

The Shah studied him for a moment, then nodded. "You speak with courage. I won't punish you, but I won't let you live here freely either. If you wish to stay, you will learn your keep. You may watch the palace geese."

And so, Hasan became the royal goose keeper.

One day, as Princess Peri strolled through the garden, her gaze fell upon the goose keeper napping beneath a tree. She stepped closer, and her heart skipped.

She knew that face. That posture. That peaceful calm. Even beneath the sheep's hide, she recognized him: it was Hasan, her match, her warrior, her promised one.

Peri said nothing. She turned quickly and ran to her chambers, her heart pounding.

From that day forward, she grew quiet and sad. She no longer danced or laughed. The queen noticed and asked her gently:

"My daughter, what troubles you?"

"Nothing, Mother," Peri replied. "I'm only… tired."

But the queen insisted, and the Shah soon grew impatient. "If my daughter is unhappy, perhaps it is time to marry her off. Let her choose a husband, as is our custom."

In that land, princesses chose their husbands by standing on a balcony and throwing an apple to the man who won their heart.

So, the Shah summoned every noble and warrior to pass below her window. One by one, they walked past, but Peri dropped no apple. The Shah grew irritated.

"Why haven't you chosen anyone?" he asked.

"The one I am waiting for," said Peri softly, "has not yet come."

Finally, the royal Vizir spoke. "There is one man who hasn't walked beneath the balcony. It was the bald goose keeper."

The Shah frowned but allowed it. Hasan, still wearing his disguise, was called forth.

As soon as he passed below, Peri dropped the apple.

Hasan caught it gently, kissed it, and placed it over his heart.

The Shah was furious.

"You choose a beggar? A bald goose keeper?" he thundered. "Then be gone!"

With that said, Hasan and Peri were cast out of the palace. But neither was sad. They settled in a small village nearby, living simply but happily, as husband and wife.

The Battle of Kings and Chains of Fire

However, after Hasan and Peri had begun their quiet life together, distant thunder echoed from the north. It was a drum of war.

Word had reached a powerful foreign Shah that the Frankish princess had married a no-name traveler, rejecting a royal suitor who had long desired her. Insulted and enraged, he gathered a vast army and marched toward the Frankish kingdom to demand revenge.

The Frankish king, now old, bitter, and still embarrassed by Peri's choice, had no strength to fight back. His people panicked. No knight, no commander, no prince in the land dared to challenge the mighty invading army. Except one.

Hasan heard the rumors in the village square. He stood up, kissed Peri's forehead, and said, "It's time."

He returned to the palace, stood before the throne, and bowed. "Let me defend your kingdom, Your Majesty. Let me fight for your people."

The Shah pale with fear, had no other option. "Go," he said. "If you return victorious, I will welcome you and my daughter back with honor."

Hasan strapped on the rusty sword, the one he had never taken off his belt, and rode out alone toward the enemy.

The enemy laughed when they saw him: one man, no army, facing thousands.

But they stopped laughing when Hasan pulled two enormous chains from his saddlebag. With a strength that no one could explain, he spun the chains above his head and charged into battle like a storm of iron.

For forty days and forty nights, the battlefield shook with the fury of war. Hasan struck down enemy after enemy, building mountains from the bodies of soldiers. But the enemy's numbers seemed endless.

Seeing this, the rival Shah summoned his secret weapon: witches and sorcerers, dark-hearted women who promised to use spells to bring Hasan down.

"If you succeed," said the Shah "I will pay you in gold, weight for weight."

An old witch stepped forward. "Give me ten of your strongest warriors," she cackled. "I will deliver Hasan to you by nightfall."

She placed them in a large clay pot, climbed in herself, and flew like a shadow toward Hasan's village. By dusk, she had arrived.

In town, she disguised herself as a beggar woman and limped toward Peri's home. When the princess stepped onto the balcony, the woman bowed low.

"Blessed daughter," she wheezed. "Is it true your husband saved the kingdom? Where does his power come from?"

Peri, proud but naive, answered softly, "It's not his chains or his swordsmanship. it is the rusty sword at his side. While he wears it, he cannot be defeated."

The witch's eyes gleamed. That night, she and her hidden warriors snuck into Hasan's tent. While he slept, they slipped the sword from his belt, and a deep spell fell over him. Hasan sank into a slumber so deep that he couldn't be woken.

Bound in ropes, Hasan and Peri were thrown into the clay pot and carried across the skies to the rival king.

Peri was thrown into the palace harem. Hasan was locked in the darkest dungeon, still asleep, unmoving.

But far away, in the mountains of the Deevs, the eldest gray Deev awoke with a jolt. Blood was dripping from the dagger Hasan had given him. Something was wrong.

He summoned his brothers, and soon the skies above the Frankish kingdom darkened as the Deevs formed a ring around the city, their towering bodies like living mountains.

The Frankish Shah trembled in fear. He sent messengers, but none dared approach the deevs.

Then one of them, Hasan's Deev-brother, stepped forward and roared:

"O son of man do not fear. Just answer one question: Where is our brother Hasan?"

The Shah stutteringly told them all he knew.

With a thunderous cry, the Deevs turned and marched on the enemy kingdom. In hours, they surrounded the city. The rival Shah seeing them descend from the skies like shadows of doom, fell to his knees.

The Deevs gave a final warning:

"Return Hasan and the princess unharmed, or we will turn your kingdom to dust."

Frightened beyond measure, the Shah ordered their release. Peri came out first, weeping with relief. But Hasan was still deep in enchanted sleep.

The princess cried out, "They stole his rusty sword! Until it is returned, he will not wake."

The eldest Deev growled and vanished into a cloud of wind. Moments later, he returned, holding the stolen sword.

He tied it around Hasan's waist, and then, Hasan sneezed and opened his eyes. The chains of sleep were broken. That night, the Deevs and humans celebrated together. Music echoed through the mountains, and fires lit the sky. Hasan and Peri returned home with honor, no longer castaways but heroes beloved by all.

A Kingdom Reunited

With Hasan awake and the enemy defeated, the Frankish kingdom breathed freely again. For the first time in many moons, there was no fear in the air, only music, laughter, and the scent of blooming citrus trees.The Deevs, towering like mountains on the horizon, bid farewell to their human brother.

"You have no need of us now," said the eldest gray Deev, his voice like distant thunder. "But know this, Hasan: should the winds ever carry your cry again, we will return."

With that, the Deevs vanished into the clouds, never to be seen again but always remembered.

The Frankish Shah kept his word. He invited Hasan and Peri back into the palace with honor. He embraced them both, no longer a stubborn ruler, but a softened father, changed by the courage and love he had witnessed.

"I judged you by your clothes, your past, and your name," he told Hasan. "But now I see what truly matters: the strength of your heart and the loyalty of your soul."

He announced a grand wedding, even greater than the first. It was a symbol of peace, unity, and forgiveness. For seven days and seven nights, the kingdom rejoiced.

Hasan ruled by Peri's side with wisdom and justice. He was not just remembered as the prince with the rusty sword, but as the man who was wise enough to follow his father's strange advice, who honored a promise, and who fought not for glory, but for those he loved.

The rusty sword was never polished. It hung in the hall, untouched. Not as a weapon of war, but as a lasting symbol of wisdom and restraint.

True strength is not found in polished armor or shining titles. It reveals itself in moments of doubt, in battles fought for love, in loyalty that holds strong through fear and failure

Ohay and Ahmed

The Boy and the Sea

ong ago, in a time so ancient it is nearly forgotten, there lived a poor man with nothing to his name. Every day, he walked down to the shore of the Caspian Sea and cast his fishing net. If he caught anything, he would sell the fish and scrape by, barely enough to live.

For many years, the man had no children. But one day, his prayers were answered: a baby boy was born, and he named him Ahmed.

Years passed, and when Ahmed turned fourteen, his father sat him down and said:

"My son, I've lived my whole life in poverty. It is because I never learned to read or write. I spent days fishing, and now that I've grown old, I no longer have the strength for even that. We've fallen into true hardship. I do not want you to live the same way. You need to learn a trade, build a better life, and escape the hardship I've known."

Ahmed did not argue.

"Whatever you say, Father. I will do as you wish."

His father's heart filled with joy.

"Well-done, my son. Prepare for a journey, tomorrow we'll go search for a wise teacher who can teach you the sciences and crafts.

The next morning, they woke before sunrise. The sky had barely begun to blush with color. They packed a small bundle: a piece of bread and some dried fish and set off on foot.

They walked for days, passing villages and towns, but nowhere could they find a skilled teacher.

Finally, exhausted, they stopped at a forest spring to rest. The father said:

"Let's eat, son. We are tired and hungry."

They shared their bread and fish and drank the cool water from the spring. The father leaned back and sighed:

"Ohay, what delicious water!"

The words had barely left his lips when the water churned and out rose a towering man with a booming voice.

"Who called me?"

Ahmed's father froze in shock, speechless. After a moment, he stammered:

"I did not call anyone. Who are you?"

"Did not you just say 'Ohay'?"

"Yes, but I was just admiring the water!"

The man narrowed his eyes.

"Ohay is my name. You called me, so here I am. Now tell me, what are you doing here?"

Realizing what had happened, the father explained:

"We came to rest. We've traveled far. I am searching for a teacher to educate my son."

Ohay's eyes sparkled.

"Well, you will not find a better teacher than me! Leave your son with me, I will teach him everything I know. Come back in one hundred days, and he will have all the secrets of knowledge in his pocket."

What more could a father want? Overjoyed, he thanked Ohay, begging him to care for Ahmed as if he were his own.

Ohay nodded kindly.

"Do not worry. Not a hair on his head will be harmed. When you return, just drink from this spring and call my name and I will bring your son to you."

The father kissed Ahmed goodbye and urged him to obey his new teacher in all things. Then he turned and walked away.

Ohay took Ahmed's hand, muttered a spell, and both vanished into the spring.

The Red Garden and the Forbidden Door

When Ahmed opened his eyes, he was standing in front of a grand fortress. Strangely, he and his clothes were perfectly dry, as if they hadn't just plunged into a spring. Curious and confused, he looked around but asked no questions.

Ohay led him through the golden gates and into a small chamber.

"This will be your room," he said. Then, without another word, he turned and left.

Ahmed's curiosity got the better of him. He stepped outside and began to explore the fortress grounds. What he saw left him speechless.

The walls of the fortress were made of bricks of gold and silver, rising high into the sky. Everything sparkled with gems and pearls, so bright it made his eyes ache.

He wandered into a garden and was stunned. Every tree, bush, and flower was red. Deep crimson, bright scarlet, dark ruby — nothing grew in any other color.

Ahmed stared in awe, but a strange chill crept over him. Something about it did not feel right.

He kept exploring. In another section, he saw dozens of animals, lions, tigers, bears, wolves, foxes, jackals; and even snakes slithered through the grass. It felt more like a cursed zoo than a living garden.

As he walked farther, he came upon a terrifying sight: a blazing inferno. Fire and smoke rose to the sky, but nothing burned. It was just... there. Alive. Breathing.

Frightened now, Ahmed fled to the back of the fortress, where he found the sea stretching endlessly. A lonely ship floated at the shore, empty and still.

Uneasy, Ahmed thought:

"Maybe Ohay tricked my father. he is not here to teach me. He will torture me, or worse. I should escape while I can."

Without hesitation, he boarded the ship and pushed off into the open sea.

He sailed for seven days and seven nights, until the ship came to a halt before a giant wall.

This was no ordinary wall. Its base was anchored deep in the ocean, and its top reached the seventh heaven. And it was made entirely of human skulls.

As the ship drifted near, voices echoed from all sides:

"Young man, turn back! Do not step ashore! Ohay will destroy you like he destroyed us. We were once like you, young and full of hope. He lured us into his fortress and killed us one by one. This wall is our grave."

"If he catches you, he will ask where you were headed. Do not tell him you were running away! Say you were sailing for fun. That is the only way he will not harm you."

"But listen, if you want to escape, there's only one way. The fortress holds a secret; it's a magic, and a weakness; only his daughter knows. If you can win her trust and learn the secret, you might survive. If not... you will join us."

Suddenly, the sea began to roar. Waves churned. And from the depths rose Ohay's head; giant, furious, and dripping with saltwater.

Ahmed did not flinch.

"I was just bored," he said calmly. "You left me alone, so I took a ride on the sea to clear my head."

Hearing this, Ohay relaxed. He reached out, took Ahmed by the hand, and brought him back to the fortress.

"I have forty rooms in this palace," Ohay said kindly. "When you are bored, feel free to open a few. Little by little, you can explore the whole place. Here, take these keys to thirty-nine of the rooms. But the fortieth, you must never enter."

Ahmed nodded, accepted the keys, and waited until Ohay was out of sight.

Then he began opening the rooms.

Every door revealed unimaginable wealth: piles of gold, glittering jewels, rare silks, enchanted trinkets. Not even a shah's treasure could compare.

By the end of a few days, he had opened thirty-nine rooms. All that remained was the mysterious fortieth door.

He stood before it, hesitating.

"What could possibly be inside?" he thought. "Why hide this one room from me? What secret is he keeping?"

His curiosity exploded. He broke the lock and stepped inside.

The room was unlike anything he had seen. Everything was velvety black. The carpets were thick and dark. The walls, the curtains, even the dishes were made from black agate. Only the diamonds scattered throughout gave off any light.

At the far end of the room, on a black marble throne, lay a girl so beautiful that her face shimmered like a star.

As Ahmed entered, she lifted her head and wiped away tears. She had been crying.

The Daughter of Ohay and the Secret of the Fortress

The girl on the throne looked up, her eyes red from weeping, but her face glowed with such beauty that Ahmed forgot to breathe. She was like a light in the darkness, brighter than the diamonds around her. For a long moment, neither of them spoke.

At last, Ahmed found his voice.

"Who are you?" he asked, his words soft with wonder. "And why are you locked away in this place, dressed in sorrow?"

The girl sat up slowly, her voice quiet and calm, yet full of pain.

"O, brave young man," she said. "Many heroes have stood where you stand now, brave warriors, clever men, and proud sons of the great kings. But none of them ever heard what I am about to tell you, because you are different. I see kindness and courage in your eyes. I will share my story."

She stood and walked toward him, the black folds of her gown trailing behind her like shadows.

"I am Ohay's daughter. This fortress belongs to my father, a powerful sorcerer. Everything here is enchanted or cursed. The gold? Cursed. The garden? Fed by blood. The animals? Once were human. The fire? Born from the cries of the dying. And the sea? It is filled with the tears of those my father tricked."

Ahmed's stomach turned, but he said nothing.

"Each time he lures a new victim," she continued, "he casts a spell on me and locks me here. I dress in black and mourn for the souls he destroys. That is why this room is full of darkness."

Then her voice softened.

"But now you are here. And for the first time in years, I have hope. If you help, trust me, then I will help you survive."

Ahmed nodded, his voice steady.

"Tell me what I need to do."

The girl leaned in and whispered:

"My father will teach you one spell every day for ninety-nine days. On the hundredth day, he will test you. If you pass, even if you know every secret, he will kill you."

"Those who fail completely, he lets go, thinking them as useless. But those who remember some spells, he turns them into beasts or insects. The same animals you already saw."

"Your only chance is to pretend to be a fool. Act like you remember nothing. Let him believe you've learned nothing at all."

Ahmed's heart pounded, but he nodded.

"I will do exactly as you say."

And so, the days passed.

Each morning, Ohay taught Ahmed a new magical art: how to become a bird, how to vanish into smoke, how to walk on water, how to control the wind. Ahmed listened, learned, and memorized, but then made sure to appear confused and forgetful.

On the hundredth day, Ohay stood before him, his eyes burning with suspicion.

"Tell me," he growled, "what is the spell to become a hawk?"

"Hmm… I do not remember," Ahmed stammered.

"Then the fire spell?"

"Completely gone from my head."

"You miserable fool!" Ohay roared. "I wasted a hundred days on you for nothing!"

He struck Ahmed in anger, cursed him, and dragged him back to the spring. As he did, Ahmed's father arrived, just as instructed.

The old man bent to the water, drank, and whispered, "Ohay."

Ohay emerged from the water holding Ahmed in his grasp.

"Here's your son," he grumbled. "The biggest idiot I've ever met. I couldn't teach him a single thing. Take him and go. He is useless."

The old man apologized and thanked Ohay at the same time, and led Ahmed away, his heart heavy.

But Ahmed? He could barely contain his joy.

When they had walked some distance, Ahmed said:

"Father, walk ahead. I will catch up."

Too tired to argue, the old man agreed. Ahmed ducked behind a bush, muttered a spell, and transformed into a limping partridge. He hopped out, wobbling in front of his father.

"Aha!" said the old man. "Dinner!"

He lunged, but the partridge slipped away.

Just then, Ahmed stepped out again, laughing.

"Oh, Father. You couldn't even catch a limping bird?"

The old man scowled.

"That is not funny, young man. We need food, and you, after all this, what good are you?"

Ahmed grinned.

"Father, listen. I learned everything. Every secret. But I fooled Ohay into thinking I was useless. Watch."

He whispered another spell and became a sleek black stallion.

"Sell me at the market," he said. "But do not sell the bridle. No matter what anyone offers, the bridle stays with you."

The old man stared in awe but did as instructed by his son.

The stallion was so beautiful that buyers crowded the market to fight for him. One man finally paid a full hundred coins, but the old man kept the bridle and returned home, where Ahmed was waiting, safe and smiling.

They lived comfortably for a while, until the money ran out.

Ahmed changed again, this time into an even more stunning horse. His father took him to the market once more.

But this time, a tall, thin *dervish*, gentle-voiced and flattering, begged the old man to sell the bridle too. The old man, hypnotized by sweet words, finally gave in.

What a mistake he made, because that dervish was Ohay in disguise.

He yanked the bridle, dragged the horse back to the fortress, and threw it at his daughter's feet.

"Guard this beast!" he spat. "I'm going for my sword. This time I will finish him for good."

But the girl recognized that it was Ahmed, and now the stakes were higher than ever.

The Chase Through Magic and Shadows

As soon as Ohay disappeared into the fortress to get his sword, his daughter rushed to the stallion, her eyes wide with fear and love.

"Ahmed," she whispered, gently stroking his mane. "I know it is you. I've missed you every day. My father going to kill you. He will not show mercy this time."

She loosened the bridle ever so slightly and leaned close.

"When he returns, shake your head hard and the bridle will slip off. The moment you are free, run. Run fast. Do not look back."

Ahmed's dark eyes blinked with understanding. The girl stepped away just in time.

Ohay stormed back in, saber gleaming in his hand, face twisted with rage.

"So, young fool," he growled, raising his sword. "You tricked me once, but you will not do it again."

But before the blade could fall, Ahmed shook his head violently. The bridle slipped off, hitting the floor with a thud. In a flash, he spoke the ancient spell and transformed into a swift red deer.

He bounded from the room in a blur of motion, his hooves barely touching the ground as he darted through the fortress gates and into the wilderness.

Ohay let out a furious cry and slammed his sword into the stone floor. Then he muttered a dark spell, slammed his staff, and became a hunter, bow in hand, arrows at his side. The chase began.

Over hills and beneath stars, they ran. Ahmed, the deer, leaped across boulders and creeks, while Ohay, the hunter, was never far behind, loosing arrows that barely missed their mark.

When Ahmed felt his strength begin to fade, he ran to a mountain spring, whispered a spell, and dove in, emerging as a golden fish, scales glimmering in the sunlight.

Ohay arrived moments later, scowled, and became a fisherman. With a flick of his wrist, he cast a net.

Ahmed dodged once. Twice. But he knew the old sorcerer would not give up.

So, he whispered another spell and became a golden apple, sinking to the bottom of the spring, hiding among the stones.

Ohay pulled up an empty net, cursed, then reached into his sack and tossed in a magic chest. The chest opened, sucking in the water and revealing the apple. But before he could grab it, the apple rolled out, and in its place, a gray sparrow shot into the sky.

The chase continued in the air.

Ahmed flapped his wings furiously, darting through clouds and mountain wind. But behind him soared a giant falcon, talons gleaming, eyes locked on its prey.

The sparrow dove toward a field and turned into a handful of millet, scattering into the tall grass.

Ohay shrieked with rage and slammed into the earth, becoming a chicken, a monstrous, wild-eyed bird, pecking madly at every grain.

One by one, the millet disappeared beneath his beak… until only one tiny seed remained. That last grain had rolled under his foot, out of sight.

And just as the chicken bent down for the final bite, a wolf leapt from the shadows.

With one snap of its sharp jaws, the wolf tore the chicken apart, feathers flying into the wind.

The wolf stood still. Silence fell. Then its body shimmered, and in its place, breathing hard, stood Ahmed, victorious. Ohay was gone.

The Oath, the Journey, and the Trial of the Three Apples

After the final battle, as Ahmed caught his breath and wiped the dust from his face, one thought rose above the rest: "She saved me." The daughter of Ohay had given him the secret to survive, and her courage had helped him escape a cruel fate.

He remembered her tears, her voice, her strength. And he remembered his promise.

"If she accepts me," Ahmed whispered to the wind, "I will return, and ask her to marry me."

And so, he did. Ahmed made his way back to the fortress. He stepped through the gates and walked straight to the fortieth room.

It was no longer dark. The walls glowed with soft light, the floor was covered in fine carpets, and the heavy gloom was gone. But there, sitting silently on a cushion, was the girl, Ohay's daughter, dressed head to toe in black.

Ahmed entered quietly.

"Why are you still in mourning?" he asked. "The fortress shines, the curse is broken."

She looked up with tired eyes.

"You are right, Ahmed. My father was cruel, but he was still my father. I rejoice that you are free, but I had to grieve for my loss."

Then she stood and walked into the next room. When she returned, she wore a dress embroidered with gold and bright threads, her hair braided in ribbons of red and silver. She looked radiant, like the morning sun after a long storm.

"Now," she said, smiling gently, "you may ask."

Ahmed dropped to one knee.

"Will you be my wife?"

She did not answer right away. Instead, she looked him in the eyes and said:

"Not yet, because long ago, I made a vow: I would marry no man unless he uncovered the secret of the White Deev's enchanted apples. It is a riddle no one has solved, and I cannot break my word."

Ahmed did not get discouraged.

"Then I will find the answer, even if it costs me my life."

She touched his hand and nodded.

"Then go. And may fortune walk with you."

The Last Riddle

As soon as Ahmed left, the girl turned into a bird and, in the blink of an eye, flew to the forest he had spent many days trying to reach. There, she transformed again, and this time into a fairy of breathtaking beauty. In this form, she met Ahmed and asked,

"Young man, may Allah forgive my curiosity, but where are you from, and where are you headed?"

Ahmed replied reluctantly,

"I'm lost. I wandered into this forest by accident."

She smiled.

"Oh, Ahmed, do not hide anything from me. I am the daughter of a mighty and noble shah. I know all the secrets and mysteries of this world. I know who you are, where you are going, and why. The daughter of Ohay wants revenge for her father's death, and that is why she sent you on a journey from which no one returns. Do not fall under her spell. Turn back while you still can."

But Ahmed stood firm.

"O fairest of the fair! I gave my word to the daughter of Ohay, and even if it costs me my life, I must uncover the secret of the magical apples."

She tried again.

"Perhaps you are afraid to lose her. But why choose her over me? Come with me to my father's lands. He is old and needs a successor. You can marry me and rule his kingdom."

Ahmed shook his head.

"O beautiful fairy, I desire nothing but to keep my promise. I will marry only the daughter of Ohay."

With those words, he continued without once looking back. But just a short distance later, the girl changed her form again, and this time into a towering warrior.

Ahmed, deep in thought, barely noticed anything ahead. His mind wandered to his father, likely waiting alone in their little cottage, and to the daughter of Ohay, left behind in the fortress.

Suddenly, he looked up and froze. A massive warrior, tall as a plane tree, was blocking the path. In each hand, the giant held seven millstones, tossing them around as if they were prayer beads.

"Who are you, boy, and where are you headed?" the warrior growled.

"I'm searching for the secret of the magical apples," Ahmed answered humbly.

The warrior laughed.

"Poor fool! A warrior like me couldn't solve that mystery, and you, a mere child, think you can?"

Ahmed shrugged.

"If I fail, I fail. I am ready to die for my promise. And you? Where are you going?"

The warrior lifted his head proudly.

"Haven't you heard of the beautiful, clever daughter of the sorcerer Ohay? I've learned that Ohay is dead, and I am on my way to marry his daughter whether she likes it or not."

Rage filled Ahmed.

"That girl is my bride! As long as I live, no one will take her away!"

The warrior's eyes bulged. Foaming at the mouth, he roared,

"How dare you! I could smash you with a single millstone!"

Seeing the warrior's fury, Ahmed drew his sword.

"If you think strength will scare me, then find out. We'll see who wins."

The girl, still disguised as the warrior, smiled to herself. Ahmed had also passed this test.

Then the warrior spoke: "It would bring me no honor to fight one so beneath my strength. Go now and may peace be with you."

With that, the warrior turned and walked away. But a few steps later, the girl changed form once more into a hideous old witch. She sat before a ruined fortress, waiting.

When Ahmed reached the fortress and saw the witch, he recoiled in horror. Her lower lip scraped the ground; her upper lip touched the sky. As soon as she saw him, her face twisted with fury.

"O son of Adam!" she screeched. "How dare you step onto my land?"

But Ahmed stood firm.

"I came in peace, old woman, there is no need to shout. I've come seeking the secret of the magical apples that belong to the White Deev."

The witch laughed cruelly.

"Many heroes have come here, as many as the hairs on your head, but none uncovered the secret. They all lost their lives. Let's see what you are made of."

She led Ahmed into a large room, left him for a moment, and returned with a golden tray holding three apples, and all the same size and color. She placed the tray on the ground and said,

"Here's your task. One apple is one year old, one is two years old, and one is three. But only I know which is which. If you guess correctly, I will reveal the secret. If not… Off with your head!

Ahmed nodded.

"Very well. Bring me a bowl of water."

The witch returned with a bowl. Ahmed placed all three apples into it. One sank to the bottom, one floated in the middle, and one rose to the top.

"Look," he said. "The apple that sank is the freshest and heaviest. It's one year old. The one in the middle is lighter, about two years old. The one floating on top is the driest and oldest, about three years old."

The witch had no choice but to admit he was right. Her face softened.

"Son, you've solved the riddle. That was the secret of the three apples. I see you are wise. I will not kill you. Go in peace."

Ahmed was about to leave when the girl returned to her proper form and called out,

"Ahmed! Ahmed…"

He turned and couldn't believe his eyes. The witch was gone. In her place stood the daughter of Ohay. He rubbed his eyes.

"Is this a dream?"

He stepped forward, stunned.

"All of that… all of it… was you?"

She nodded.

"No, Ahmed," she said. "It's not a dream. I was the witch. I was also the fairy who tried to tempt you, and the warrior with the millstones. I had to know if your heart was true. I tested you and you pass every trial."

Ahmed fell to one knee and held out the glowing stones.

"I kept my promise. Will you keep yours?"

She laughed softly, knelt beside him, and said: "Yes."

The Wedding and the Liberation of the Enchanted Ones

On their way back, they reached the fortress and lifted the spells that Ohay had cast over the people. Even the dead were brought back to life. The freed captives fell to their knees before Ahmed and his bride and said:

"You have saved us. We are ready to serve you for the rest of our days."

But Ahmed replied kindly:

"We do not ask for your servitude. I have only one request. Today we journey to my father's home, where we'll hold our wedding. Come with us. Be our guests. After the celebration, you may all go wherever your hearts lead."

From all the treasure in the fortress, Ahmed and his bride took only what was valuable and easy to carry. Then Ahmed turned to the people and said:

"Take whatever you wish, and the rest is yours."

Once again, the people praised and thanked him. Then Ahmed, his bride, and all those they had freed set off together.

They traveled for many days until they arrived at Ahmed's father's home. The poor old man saw a great crowd approaching, and at the head of it was his son, walking beside a bride as radiant as the moon. For a moment, the old man was speechless with joy. Ahmed ran to him, bowed at his feet, and kissed his hand.

His father embraced him, still in awe, and asked:

"My son, who are these people? And where have you been all this time?"

Ahmed sat beside him and told him everything that had happened since he left.

The very next day, they began preparing for the wedding. The celebration lasted forty days and forty nights. And never in anyone's lifetime had there been a wedding so grand.

Years passed. The red garden remained green, the fortress stood empty, and the sea sang only to the wind.

Ahmed and the daughter of Ohay lived in peace and harmony. Ahmed's father lived to see his son honored, not for wealth, but for his honesty, love, and compassion for others. The story ends, as all good tales must. But its echo remains, if you know how to listen.

To seek wisdom is to walk with courage, and when tested, to stand steady like a river stone, because strength alone is never enough.

The Nightingale of Hazar

The Missing Wonders

Long ago, there was a Great Shah who had the most beautiful garden anyone had ever seen. Roses spoke in fragrances, nightingales sang to one another, and crystal-clear springs murmured through the trees. The Shah had ordered trees from every corner of the world, and his garden became so lush and enchanting that it was said to contain the very soul of life.

People traveled from far and wide just to witness its beauty.

One day, three travelers came from a distant city and toured the garden with the Shah. As they left, one said:

"An incredible garden, but it is a shame Bilgeiz Hanum isn't here to see it."

The second added:

"Beautiful indeed, but where's the rose and the nightingale of Hazar, the ones kept by Bilgeiz Hanum?"

The third said:

"Wonderful, yes, but if only it had the legendary Suleimani-Arab Stallion."

These comments troubled the Shah. His Vizir noticed.

"Long live the Shah! What weighs on your heart?" he asked.

"It's the travelers' words," replied the Shah, "My garden is missing the Rose and nightingale of Hazar, the Suleimani-Arab horse and Bilgeiz Hanum herself. I must have them, no matter what."

"But my Shah," said the Vizir, "you have three sons. Call them. Order them to find these wonders. What greater purpose could there be for sons than to serve their father now?"

The Shah agreed. He summoned his sons and said:

"My sons, my garden is unmatched in all the world, but it lacks four things: the Rose and the nightingale of Hazar, the Suleimani-Arab horse and Bilgeiz Hanum. I do not know how or where, but I command you to find them, even if the sky must touch the earth, fulfill your duty, and bring honor to our name."

The three princes kissed their father's hand in respect, mounted their horses, and set off on their quest.

Through Fire for a Horse

Day after day, the three princes traveled, crossing mountains and rivers, resting at night beneath starlit skies. Eventually, they reached a crossroads where three paths diverged. There, they buried a ring beneath a large stone, agreeing that whoever returned first would come back for the others. They embraced beneath the shining sun, offered blessings for the road ahead, and each set off on a different path—one to the east, one to the west, and one toward the mountains.

After several days of travel, the youngest prince reached a city and stopped before a humble house. At the gate stood an old man.

"Kind man," said the prince, "I'm a traveler from far away. May I stay here for the night?"

"Of course," replied the old man. "A guest is a gift from God."

This old man had seen many years, endured hardship and joy, and recognized the signs of someone with a purpose. Over dinner, the prince shared about his mission to find the legendary stallion, Suleimani-Arab.

The old man grew serious.

"Son, you are brave, but many strong men have come seeking that horse. None returned. you are still young, barely more than a child. Better to turn back now."

"I made a promise to my father," the prince replied, "and I intend to keep it."

The old man sighed.

"Very well. I will tell you what I know. The horse drinks each morning from a sacred spring far from here, but the path to it lies beyond seven flaming gorges. If you can reach that spring, climb the tree beside it and hide in its branches before dawn. When the herd comes into a view, seize your moment, throw your rope true and catch the lead stallion, Suleimani-Arab. But say the exact words: 'Horse, in the name of the Prophet Suleiman, stop!' If you get them wrong, the horse will tear the tree out by its roots and crush you beneath it. And once you are on his back, ride without looking back, no matter what sounds you hear. If you turn around, you will turn to stone."

The next morning, the prince set off. In the distance, he soon saw a strange light. It grew brighter as he approached, until he realized that it was fire. The first gorge blazed like a furnace.

The heat was intense, but the prince did not hesitate. He charged straight into the flames. Thunder cracked, lightning flashed, and the ground roared like a beast. Any ordinary traveler would have turned back. But the prince pressed on, eyes fixed ahead, heart full of courage.

He passed through the first gorge. Then the second. Then the third. One by one, all seven flaming gorges. Each more fearsome than the last, but the prince never wavered, never once turned his head.

At last, he emerged onto a calm, flowering plain. In its center stood a tall tree, with a spring bubbling at its roots. Just as the old man had said.

He drank, ate a little food, then climbed the tree and waited.

At dawn, the ground trembled. Thunder rolled. Then came the herd of stallions galloping like a storm. At their front was the horse: black as night, powerful as the sea, eyes burning like coals.

The prince held his breath. When the stallion lowered its head to drink, he threw the rope and leapt.

"Horse, in the name of the Prophet Suleiman, stop!"

The stallion froze mid-leap. He had heard the name, and he could not resist.

The prince gripped tightly and swung onto the horse's back. Screeches and cries echoed behind him: "Stop him! Catch him!" but he did not look back.

The wind roared past. In just two hours, the prince returned to the city he had left five days earlier. Without pausing, he rode on to the crossroads and checked under the stone. The rings were still there, and his brothers had not returned.

He placed the rings beneath the stone on the second path and set off to find the next wonder.

Brothers, Battles, and the Beautiful Rose

After hiding the ring beneath the next stone, the youngest prince took the second road. As he traveled, days turned to weeks, with new landscapes unfolding before him. Finally, he reached a city and stopped at its edge to rest his horse.

Feeling hungry, he walked into town and stepped into a small kebab shop. As he waited for food, he glanced at the kitchen—and froze. The boy working there was no stranger. It was his middle brother.

"Brother! What happened to you?" he asked in shock.

His brother looked away, ashamed.

"I failed. I found nothing. I ran out of money and couldn't pay for lodging, so they made me work here as a kitchen boy."

The youngest prince paid off his brother's debts, bought him a new horse and travel gear, and led him back outside the city. There, he gently plucked a few strands from Suleimani-Arab's mane, blew on them, and let them go into the wind.

In an instant, the magical stallion galloped to them like a lightning bolt.

The brothers rode together, returning to the crossroads. The ring was still beneath the third stone, so the oldest brother had not yet come back.

"Stay here," the youngest said. "I will go after him."

He followed the third road. After a long journey, he came to a city unlike any other. At its heart stood a towering palace, and on the balcony sat the most dazzling woman he had ever seen.

Her name was Bilgeiz Hanum.

But below her palace, a strange scene unfolded: a crowd of young men stomped through mud up to their knees, mixing clay like slaves. They were ragged, barefoot, and silent.

And among them, the youngest prince recognized his eldest brother.

"Brother!" he cried. "What is going on?"

"She is Bilgeiz Hanum," his brother answered grimly. "Many princes came to ask for her hand. But she declared: only a man who can defeat her in wrestling may marry her. All who lose must stay and mix mud for the rest of their lives. I was one of them…"

"Then I will challenge her," said the youngest.

"Do not be foolish! She's stronger than all of us. Do not throw your life away."

But the prince was determined. He looked up and called:

"Bilgeiz Hanum! Come down and fight me!"

She laughed.

"Look at these men below, each one a warrior, now mixing mud. I do not want to see you crushed. Go home."

"No more talk," he said. "Come down and fight."

"Oh, poor boy," she mocked. "You still smell of your mother's milk. I am warning you that I fight to win. If I beat you, I take your head."

"And if I win?" he asked.

"Then I will be yours, faithful and true, in heart, soul, in joy and sorrow, for all my days."

They wrestled for three days and three nights, neither gaining the upper hand. But on the fourth morning, with one final burst of strength, the prince threw her to the ground.

She looked up at him and whispered:

"You won. I accept your terms of the deal."

He freed all the defeated contenders from the mud. He gathered what he came for: the Nightingale of Hazar, the enchanted Rose, the mighty stallion, and now, Bilgeiz Hanum.

Together with his two brothers, they returned to the crossroads, set up camp, cooked, feasted, and rested before the long road back. But that night, while the youngest prince slept soundly, the two elder brothers lay awake, plotting.

They were terrified of facing their father empty-handed and jealous of their younger brother's success.

So, under the cover of night, they tied him up and threw him into a deep well.

Betrayal and Return

As the youngest prince lay in the well, unconscious and bound, his brothers packed up camp at dawn. They loaded the enchanted Rose, the nightingale, and Bilgeiz Hanum onto camels and set off.

Before leaving, Bilgeiz Hanum asked,

"Where is your brother?"

The brothers replied,

"He left during the night to deliver the good news to our father. He wanted to surprise him."

Suspicious, but silent, Bilgeiz Hanum said nothing. But the magic stallion, Suleimani-Arab, was not fooled. No matter how hard the brothers tried, he would not let them ride or touch him. Furious, they left him behind and chose a different horse from the caravan.

They returned home, presenting everything they had taken, from the singing nightingale to the glowing Rose, to their father, the Great Shah.

The Great Shah was thrilled.

"But where is my youngest son?" he asked.

"He failed," the brothers said. "He was too ashamed to return."

The Great Shah believed them and said no more. Bilgeiz Hanum was given royal quarters in the palace, but she remained in mourning, silent and distant. She refused to speak of marriage or provide the Rose with a nightingale to anyone.

Meanwhile, far away, the youngest prince began to regain his consciousness at the bottom of the well, the chill seeping from the stones into his bones. Morning sunlight touched his face, waking him.

As he opened his eyes, pain and confusion set in. Then came the memory of betrayal.

"So, this is how my brothers repay me," he whispered bitterly. "I saved them, and they reward me with a grave on the bottom of the well."

There were no footholds in the well, and no rope to climb. But he wasn't completely alone.

Above the well-paced Suleimani-Arab, his loyal horse. The stallion sniffed the air and caught the prince's scent. He circled the well nervously, snorting and pawing at the ground. Then, finding a nearby fruit tree, the horse tore down branches and dropped them into the well, one by one.

Each day, the prince fed on fruit. Each night, Suleimani-Arab slept by the well.

Then one day, a traveling caravan came through. When the merchants saw the beautiful stallion circling a well, they tried to catch it but failed. Curious, they peered inside the well and heard a voice cry out:

"Help me! I am down here!"

The merchants quickly fetched ropes and pulled the prince out. After recovering his strength, he told them everything that had happened. They were amazed and offered help, but the prince declined.

He simply plucked a few strands from Suleimani-Arab's mane, whispered thanks, and sent the horse galloping into the hills.

Then, not wanting to be recognized, he kept his head low and found work as a cook's helper at a small roadside kebab shop, just enough to stay fed and unnoticed while he watched and waited.

The Hidden Hero

Days turned into weeks. The Shah, unaware of the truth, decided it was time to marry off Bilgeiz Hanum to his eldest son, the very one who had betrayed his brother.

He sent messengers to her chamber with his command.

But Bilgeiz Hanum, dressed in black and still silent, gave a calm but firm reply:

"My true price has not yet arrived. Whoever wants to marry me must first defeat me in a contest of strength. Only then will I agree to marriage."

The Shah, confused but eager, commanded his eldest son to wrestle with her. But the prince knew full well he had no chance, he had seen her strength before. So, blaming illness, he stayed in bed.

The Shah consulted his Vizir.

"What do you make of this?"

"Long live the Great Shah," said the Vizir. "Your son is love-struck. Let's hold the wedding. Once he marry the bride, his strength will return."

The Shah agreed. Preparations for the grand wedding began with fires being lit, kettles boiled with rice and saffron, and nobles from across the land were invited.

Meanwhile, the youngest prince, still disguised as a humble cook's apprentice, watched from the shadows.

On the day of the horse-riding games and trials of strength, the city gathered to watch the riders show off their skill. The Great Shah and his court looked on from high terraces, and Bilgeiz Hanum stood silently on her balcony.

As the shop closed for the day and the kebab shop owner hurried off to watch the festival, the prince seized his moment at last. He stepped outside, pulled the stallion's hairs from his pocket, and let them float in the wind. With a thunderous whinny, Suleimani-Arab appeared in a flash, like a storm sweeping through the mountains.

The prince mounted the horse and rode into the ring of champions. His speed and grace stunned the crowd. The stallion leapt higher than any other, ran faster than the wind, and outshone every other horse and rider.

In a blur, the prince galloped across the field and, with one clean strike, fatally defeated the eldest brother.

Gasps filled the air. The Shah jumped to his feet.

"Catch him! Whoever stops this rider will get half of my land!"

Dozens of warriors charged after him.

But the prince leaned down and whispered,

"In the name of the Prophet Suleimani, fly!"

The stallion rose on his hind legs, then soared into the sky and vanished into the clouds.

The crowd fell silent. The wedding turned into a funeral. Black banners replaced festive silks. And the city mourned for forty days.

But up in her chamber, Bilgeiz Hanum smiled quietly. She had seen his face. She knew who he was. Her prince was alive and near.

The Reckoning

A whole year passed.

The cook, still unaware that his apprentice had once been a prince, often grumbled about the mysterious rider who had ruined the royal wedding.

"That rascal," he had mutter while stirring stew. "Came out of nowhere, turned the whole palace upside down! But I admit, the way he rode… now that was something."

And the apprentice would reply with a sly smile,

"What a shame I wasn't there to see him."

Time rolled on. The Shah, still determined to marry off Bilgeiz Hanum, sent word again:

"Prepare. I now give you in marriage to my second son."

As before, the princess refused to marry without a fair contest.

"Whoever wants to wed me must defeat me in a trial of strength," she declared. "That is my only condition."

Once again, the Shah's son's fake illness, afraid to face her.

The Vizir offered the same excuse:

"He is love-sick. Let the wedding go on. Once she is his, he will recover."

So, the Shah agreed. Once again, the city was dressed in silk and gold, the fires were lit, and guests poured in for another royal celebration.

And once again, as the final day of the wedding games arrived, the youngest prince made his move.

The cook left to watch the festivities. The prince stepped out, pulled the stallion's hair from his pouch, and let them fly into the wind. With a roar like thunder, Suleimani-Arab returned.

This time, the prince rode harder and faster than before, leaping into the arena like a storm. The people recognized him; how could they not?

Before anyone could stop him, he rode straight through the crowd and fatally struck the Great Shah's middle son.

The Shah stood frozen. The people screamed. But the prince galloped toward the royal terrace, reined in his steed, dismounted, and stood before his father.

The Shah's eyes widened in disbelief.

"My son? Is it you?"

The prince bowed and said calmly,

"Yes, Father. And I have come not for revenge, but for justice."

Shocked, the Shah stepped down from his throne, his face pale.

"What happened? Tell me everything."

So, the prince told his story: from the fiery valleys to the magical horse, from rescuing his brothers to their betrayal and being cast into the well. He recounted how he survived with the help of his horse and the caravan that saved him. He told the truth, plainly and without bitterness.

The Great Shah listened in silence. When the tale ended, he lowered his head in shame.

"It is not my place to judge you, my son, not after they abandoned you to death. Yet justice must be served, even if it is harsh, even if the traitor bears our blood."

After forty days of mourning for the middle son, sorrow slowly gave way to celebration. The people rejoiced, for the truth had come to light, and justice had been done. The Shah declared a wedding, and joy returned to the land like spring after a long winter.

The Shah declared:

"Let the rightful hero be crowned! Let the true wedding begin!"

The city lit up with lanterns, music, and laughter.

For forty days and forty nights, they celebrated the wedding of the youngest prince and Bilgeiz Hanum, the unmatched warrior princess.

The Garden of Wonders

To honor the hero's return and the union of love and courage, the Shah ordered a palace to be built right in the heart of his legendary garden.

The finest builders came from across the land, and soon a dazzling crystal castle stood beneath the sky, surrounded by whispering fountains, blossoming trees, and fragrant air that smelled of roses and rain.

Inside this paradise lived:

The youngest prince, now a man praised in every corner of the land, is known for his bravery and his heart. Bilgeiz Hanum, proud and radiant, was still unmatched in wisdom and strength. The magical Rose of Hazar was planted in the garden's center. The Nightingale of Hazar, whose songs at dawn made even the oldest trees tremble. Lastly, Suleimani-Arab, the thunder-hearted stallion, whose hooves never knew fear.

The garden was complete.

There was no corner where envy could hide, no wind that carried sorrow. The scent of justice lingered longer than perfume, and the people told their children:

"Let this garden remind you: truth cannot be buried, and courage always finds its way home."

And so, they lived with joy, ruled with wisdom, and one day, returned to the earth like all who came before and after.

The brave, the loyal, and the wise will drink sweet water in the end, while the deceitful are left with dust in their mouths.

But the story did not end.

Because...

From the sky fell three apples:

One for the teller of this tale, one for the listener with an open heart, and one for the soul who believes that in every dark valley, there waits a songbird.

Glossary of Cultural Terms

Arshin - An old unit of length used in the East, approximately 28 inches or 71 centimeters.

Ashug – a traditional bard or troubadour, often traveling and performing songs that blend poetry, storytelling, and folk wisdom.

Baba – A respectful and affectionate term meaning "father" or "old man" in Azerbaijan and other regional languages

Bey – A chieftain or leader of a village or tribe; sometimes used as a title of respect.

Caravanserai – a roadside inn or rest stop used by travelers and traders along ancient trade routes like the Silk Road.

Deev (Div) – a fearsome demon or ogre from Persian and Turkic mythology. These supernatural beings often serve as enemies of heroes, representing chaos, darkness, or evil.

Dervish - A wandering ascetic or spiritual figure in Islamic tradition, known for poverty, humility, and devotion.

Hanum (Khanum) – a respectful title for a woman, like "lady" or "madam."

Hide - The skin of an animal, usually tanned and used for clothing, blankets, or other materials.

Kechal – Literally "Baldy" or "the bald boy"; a popular character in Azerbaijani folklore known for his wit and resourcefulness despite his appearance.

Khan – A title given to a ruler or nobleman, commonly used in Turkic and Mongolic cultures.

Mane - The long, thick hair growing from the neck of a horse or lion.

Saz – A long-necked string instrument used by ashiqs and folk musicians in the Caucasus, Anatolia, and Central Asia.

Shah or Padishah – a royal title meaning king or ruler, used historically across Persian, Azerbaijani, and Central Asian regions.

Staff - A long stick carried for support or as a symbol of authority or power.

Tandır -A traditional clay oven used in Azerbaijani cooking, often for baking bread or roasting meat.

Vizir – A high-ranking political advisor or minister who serves the shah or king.

About Azerbaijan

Azerbaijan is a country in the South Caucasus region, where Eastern Europe meets Western Asia. It borders the Caspian Sea to the east, Russia to the north, Georgia to the northwest, Armenia to the west, Iran to the south, and Türkiye in the southwest via the Nakhichevan exclave.

The landscape ranges from the towering Caucasus Mountains to dry steppes and fertile lowlands. Azerbaijan is home to 9 out of the 11 major climate zones in the world, making it one of the most climatically diverse countries on Earth despite its small size.

Historically, Azerbaijan has been part of several great empires, including the Persian, Arab, Seljuk, Mongol, and Russian empires. It later became part of the Soviet Union until gaining independence in 1991. The country is home to a majority Turkic-speaking Azerbaijani population and has long been a cultural crossroads along the Silk Road, blending Turkic, Persian, Caucasian, and Islamic influences.

The Azerbaijani language belongs to the Turkic language family and is spoken primarily by ethnic Azerbaijanis. It was initially written in the Perso-Arabic script, which was used widely until the early 1920s. In the late 1920s, the script was replaced with a Latin alphabet, then shifted to Cyrillic in the late 1930s under Soviet rule. After gaining independence in 1991, Azerbaijan officially returned to the Latin script.

These frequent alphabet changes disrupted generational literacy and created cultural gaps, as many older written works became inaccessible to younger readers.

A significant population of Azerbaijanis resides in Northwestern Iran, where the Perso-Arabic script continues to be used for writing Azerbaijani today.

Cities and Geographic Landmarks

Baku – The capital and largest city of Azerbaijan, located on the western shore of the Caspian Sea.

Ganja – One of the oldest cities in Azerbaijan, located in the western part of the country. Ganja has been a cultural, literary, and political center for centuries and is known as the birthplace of the great 12th-century poet Nizami Ganjavi. It played a key role in medieval trade routes and has long been associated with Azerbaijani poetry, architecture, and heroic folktales.

Tabriz – A historic city in the Azerbaijan province of Iran, Tabriz has been a major center of Turkic culture, trade, and politics for over a thousand years. Once a capital of various Persian and Turkic dynasties, it has strong cultural and linguistic ties to the Republic of Azerbaijan. Tabriz has influenced Azerbaijani music, art, literature, and storytelling traditions across the region.

Caspian Sea – The world's largest inland body of water, located between Europe and Asia. It borders five countries: Azerbaijan, Russia, Kazakhstan, Turkmenistan, and Iran. Though called a "sea," it is a large saltwater lake with no natural outlet. The Caspian Sea has shaped the history, trade, and folklore of Azerbaijan for centuries, serving as a gateway for cultural exchange along the Silk Road and appearing in many traditional stories, songs, and legends.

Lower Caucasus - The southeastern part of the Caucasus Mountain range, stretching across parts of Azerbaijan, Georgia, and Armenia. Unlike the towering peaks of the Greater Caucasus to the north, the Lower Caucasus is characterized by gentler hills, forested slopes, and rich valleys. This region has long been home to diverse cultures and languages.

About the Author

Dr. Rustam Musevi was born and raised in Baku, Azerbaijan. Now living in the United States, he is a father, grandfather, and passionate cultural storyteller devoted to preserving and sharing the tales of his youth with new generations across the globe.

A U.S. Army veteran and dentist by profession, Dr. Musevi is also a lifelong scholar. He earned his Doctor of Education by exploring the lived experiences of Azerbaijani immigrants in America, a journey that mirrors his own. Inspired by the challenge of passing down culture across languages and continents, he created *The Golden Pomegranate*, a series dedicated to bringing Azerbaijani folktales into modern English.

This volume is the first in a heartfelt series celebrating the timeless stories, wisdom, and spirit of Azerbaijan, a gift for young readers, families, and anyone who knows that a good story always finds its way home.

Volume II of The Golden Pomegranate

More timeless tales from the heart of Azerbaijan…

In the next volume, you'll journey with Malik-Mammad beneath the earth, follow Zarniyar as she matches wits with a Shah, and learn what secrets lie in The Golden Candlestick. You'll meet a master builder named Usta Abdulla, a fearless princess of Samarkand, and a humble man who speaks the truth, even to a lion.

These stories, like the ones before, come from the soul of a land where East meets West and magic lingers in the mountains.

More adventures. More wonder. More stories to share from the snow-capped peaks of the Caucasus to the waves of the Caspian Sea, where folklore still whispers on the wind, and every tale carries a piece of home.